Wyldcard Chronicles

Ty Eros

This literary work is purely from the heart, mind, soul, and life experiences of the author. Any similarities to actual persons or situations are completely coincidental.

ISBN: 0692542930
ISBN-13: 978-0692542934

DEDICATION

This book is dedicated to all my supporters and if you're reading this it includes YOU! Hold on to your dreams and don't stop fighting until you've reached your destiny!

CONTENTS

ACKNOWLEDGMENTS

So many people have come and gone since I started this journey, but I'm truly thankful for them all! Every rock in the road is meant to be a stepping stone. Remember these words as you go through life and know that everyone isn't meant to be a permanent part of your life. Thanks to all who have been there and continue to support me!

Ty Eros

PREFACE

The mind and world of author, entertainer, and entrepreneur, Ty Eros, is full of the unexpected. So we decided to write this piece to give all our fans a little sneak peek into his life. In this mix of fantasy and reality we want to give you the opportunity to get to know the man behind the stories. That said, it'll be up to you to decipher between the things that are his actual life experiences and those that are pure imagination. It's Wyldcard Entertainment so we had to bring a little fun to the party right? Well, anyway, all that being said, we thank you for your support and hope that you will enjoy every moment of this book.

<u>WELCOME TO THE CITY</u>

Finally, after years of trying to keep in touch by texting, phone calls, skype, and social media, my homeboy Sam was coming to visit me for a while. After he moved to Texas for school I got an opportunity to work for a film studio out here in Atlanta and we've kind of been kept apart by our schedules. Unfortunately, the job fell through but a couple months later I got a gig as the personal assistant to Ty Eros, the owner of Wyldcard Entertainment. I was a little nervous about it at first, being the son of two pastors and a licensed minster myself, but the pay and benefits were great and there was always lots of eye candy. Not to mention Ty was pretty sexy too, but he was off limits since he was my boss. Anyway though, my childhood friend Sam was coming into town and I couldn't wait to see him again. I had also managed to pull a few strings to help him make a few coins while he's here and hopefully that might persuade him to stay a little longer or maybe for good. I'm Devon by the way, I tend to ramble and forget things a little when I get excited, but anyway, now that the introduction is out of the way I can get back to the good stuff.

So this weekend my boss was gonna be hosting a little event and I suggested that my friend Sam be the host. Ty was a little hesitant to use him but after I showed him a few pictures on Facebook he was a little more willing and even offered to let Sam spend the weekend at the loft. It seemed like a fairly good idea to me and I'm sure Sam would prefer having a bedroom and all instead of bunking on my coach. However, I figured Ty just wanted him close so he could exam the goods before he gave the final stamp of approval. There was only was caution though, Sam didn't know I had booked him and Ty was gonna be in for a surprise if he tried to pry into those cakes. He also thought we were cousins but that was a detail I'm sure Sam and I could make work till after the event. In the meantime, I need to get my ass up and run these errands for Ty and make some phone calls to lock in our prospects for the auditions. Ty also wants me to have a backup

3

host just in case Sam doesn't meet his standards. Once they meet in person I don't believe there will be a problem though. Come to think of it the bed in that room probably needs sheets and it might need some towels in the bathroom too. I don't think there has been any sheets on that bed since the last houseguest left and Ty rarely uses that bathroom. Guess I'll do that first and then make these phone calls so I can finish telling yall about Sam and the event this weekend.

No sooner than maybe ten minutes after I finished making up the bed and got back to the office the door buzzer started to ring. The only person I was expecting was Sam and I knew it wasn't him. The one interview I'd managed to schedule wasn't until tomorrow and the UPS delivery would probably get here later this evening. So I figured that it may be some wannabe that figured out our location or something and wanted to talk. Slowly, I got up and went to the intercom, pressing the button just as the buzzer went off again.

"Hello I'm looking for 2587 N

Continental Dr, is this it?" a slightly familiar male voice said from the other end.

"Yes this is it, but this is a private residence. May I ask who or what you are looking for sir," I replied turning on my professional voice.

"I'm looking for Wyldcard Entertainment, I asked this dude in the train station how to get here," he answered.

"Damn I wish this thing had video," I said under my breath, "Come on up sir," I said, curious to see who was on the other side of the intercom and what he wanted. The voice sounded familiar but it was still usual for people to just pop up on our doorstep.

"Devon are you in there," the voice called between light taps from the knocker.

"Yea just a second," I yelled back, now really anxious to see who this was calling me by my name.

"What took you so long dude, I thought when you heard my voice you'd recognize

who I was," Sam scolded as I opened the door.

"Nigga don't come in here fussing at me and you ain't even got your foot in the door yet," I snapped back, relieved and happy to see him but curious at how he'd gotten here.

"I'm in here now what," Sam retorted, pushing me out of the way and stepping inside.

"So you starting shit already huh... anyway what are you doing here? I thought your bus didn't get here till four," I inquired, paying no mind to the shit he was talking.

"Nah I took the overnight so we got here at like eight this morning. Then it took me about an hour or so to find this place and I was downstairs pressing buttons for like five minutes before I finally got you," he explained.

"Oh ok, but why didn't you just call me instead of going through all that? I could've

just come got you from the bus station like I was supposed to anyway," I stated, reaching for the large duffle bag hanging from his shoulder.

"Yea well, I kind of wanted to surprise you and my phone died when I got on the train," Sam replied, pushing my hand away.

"Ok, well... I'm glad you made here safe, now let me show you where you'll be sleeping," I said pointing towards the hallway, "The first door to your left is the bathroom, the one next two it is the laundry room, the last door is Ty's room, and this one will be yours. Ty is rarely here outside of business hours unless there's something going on so you don't have to worry much about him," I added.

Ok and yea I made it here safe but there's some bold, thirsty ass niggas out here," he stated, stepping through the door I'd just opened and throwing the duffle bag down next to the bed.

"Well can you blame them?" I asked,

smirking a little.

"Yea, yea, yea wipe that grin off your face nigga. I don't think that shit is funny at all," he snapped as he peeled out of his shirt.

"Maybe not, but when you look like that and got ass like this it's not hard to attract attention," I laughed, playfully smacking his ass a couple times.

"Whatever, I'm used to getting looks but these dudes are like vultures going after a fresh kill man," he stated, continuing to undress.

"Well you are fresh meat," I joked.

"Anyway, where's that bathroom again? I'd like to shave and take a shower before I go get a bite to eat," Sam inquired.

"It's up the hall, but I need to get you some towels and where exactly are you planning on eating," I asked.

"I saw a lil café about a block down from here while I was walking," he answered.

"Oh ok, maybe I'll go with you, but first let me go get these towels for you," I said as I dashed out of the room.

Moments later I returned to find Sam laying on the bed in his boxers. Naturally my eyes when straight to the thick bulge between his legs and I couldn't help but notice how muscular he'd gotten. In my mind I could see myself ripping those boxers off and reacquainting myself with that thick, long dick of his. For a second our eyes met and I could tell that he was thinking the same thing but I didn't want to seem thirsty. Especially since he was already feeling some type of way about being hit on by the locals. However, he was six feet of muscle and chocolate covered sexiness and it was getting hard to resist.

"So are you going to give me the towels, suck my dick, or just stand there and stare at me," Sam asked, breaking the silence.

"Oh my bad... you've gotten a lot bigger since the last time I saw you... here you go. The bathroom is the last door to your right since you're coming from the opposite

direction," I answered, reiterating where the bathroom was before walking away.

I went back to my desk and proceeded to do some work but my thoughts were flooded with the image of Sam and that thick dick innocently staring at me. Then I remembered that I had to pretend that he was my cousin all weekend, but this was going to be a lot harder now that he was here. I also had to persuade him to be the host for this event Ty was having. Hopefully I hadn't put my foot in my mouth by speaking too soon. See if you couldn't tell already Sam is sort of conservative and not really into the gay scene, but maybe once I tell him that it's a paid gig he'll at least consider it. Not to mention I hadn't even begun looking for a backup and I still needed to call and setup the rest of the interviews and auditions for tomorrow. Ty would probably kill me if he knew how far behind I was with the planning especially since we were two days away from the event. On the other hand, I had gotten most of the guest confirmed, the supplies and party favors had been ordered and due for delivery later *today, I'm going pick up the drinks this afternoon, and I'm getting on the phone right now to confirm these last two auditions. I just hope I'm not too late to book these guys and in my mind I was praying that Ty didn't walk through that door and catch me doing shit that should've been done last week.*

"Hello," the first caller answered after the phone rang for what seemed like a year.

"Hey may I speak Darian," I asked in my most professional tone.

"This is Darian," the guy responded.

"Ok great, this is Devon, Ty Eros' assistant, we got your email and we wanted to setup an interview with you to possibly book you as one of the dancers for our event this weekend. Does ten tomorrow morning work for you? I know it's last minute, but we received a lot of submissions and I'm doing my best to go through them all and contact the ones Ty really liked," I stated, trying to add a little empathetic pressure in hopes of sealing the deal.

"Yea I can definitely do that, I've actually been hoping you guys would call me," Darian replied.

"Great, so I'll put you down for ten in the morning, do not be late and remember to bring your driver's license or ID, and be prepared to audition if the interview goes well," I instructed.

"Don't worry I'll be there and ready bro," he stated anxiously.

"Ok I'll see you in the morning," I said breathing a sigh of relief as I hung up, now I just had to get the other one locked in.

Ten minutes later I'd secured all the interviews and shot a couple emails to some friends for some favors just in case. I think Ty will be happy with the selections though and we probably won't even need the backup plan. However, there was one issue that I discovered while I was emailing my industry contacts. The delivery that was supposed to happen today was delayed and wouldn't arrive till tomorrow or Friday morning. There's not really a whole I could do about that though so I'm not stressing. I could hear the faint sound of the shower running in the background and I figured I might as well go head and talk to Sam now. I had to psych myself up a little but I had a feeling he'd be ok with it.

"Hey Sam can I come in, I need to ask you something right quick," I shouted, as I stepped up to the door.

"Yea it's open bruh," he yelled back from the other side.

"Damn bruh, it's like a sauna in this bitch," I exclaimed as the steam smacked me in the face when I opened the door.

"It's not really that hot, but what was so important that you had to see me naked," Sam laughed.

"I've seen you naked before so that's nothing new, but I wanted to know if you would rather order pizza for lunch and we can go out for dinner after I've finished running the last of my errands for the day. I figured since you just got here I could be a little

selfish and steal some one on one time with you," I said, carefully choosing my words.

"Ok that's cool, but what's really on your mind?" he inquired, seeing straight through me.

"Well... is it really that obvious?" I asked.

"D I've known you since we were five bruh, you think I wouldn't know when there's something on your mind? Now what's wrong Diggy boy?" he pressed.

"You know I hate that name right?" I stated dryly.

"Yea I do, now spit it out," Sam urged.

"Well I kind of convinced Ty to give you a job this weekend but he wants to meet you first," I answered hesitantly.

"Is that so? Exactly what kind of job is it?" he asked, eyeing me with that soul-jerking stare of his.

"Well... it's a freak party Friday night

and I suggested that you be the host. Now before you get upset I was only trying to help and I knew you could use the money. All you have to do is welcome the guests, facilitate the activities, be sexy, and the rest will take care of itself," I explained, nervously twirling my fingers around.

"How much money are we talking?"

"The pay is three hundred bucks for the event, plus any tips you get during the night."

"Ok I'll do it on two conditions, well... maybe three," Sam stated.

"Humm ok... I can't guarantee that Ty will go for it, but I'm listening," I said, watching attentively as the water cascaded down Sam's body.

"Well just listen and we'll cross that bridge when we get to it," he replied.

"Aight, I'm listening," I reiterated with a little more emphasis.

"Ok, well first I don't want anybody feeling me up or trying anything sexual unless

15

I allow it."

"Ok."

"Next I'm not wearing no lil tight skimpy outfit or walking around naked."

"Humm... ok."

"Last you need to get over here and suck this dick till I bust on your face. I haven't busted a nut in about two weeks so if you want me to do you a favor you need to do one for me," Sam ordered.

"Ok well, the first one is understandable and it is part of our policy, no means no. The second one is a little debatable, but I want you to be comfortable so we can go shopping for an outfit..."

"Uh huh so you gon suck this dick or what nigga," he snapped, cutting me off.

"Well I was getting to that but there's something else I need to tell you," I said.

"Ok what else you got me into," Sam asked, leaning against the wall and stroking

his dick.

"Nothing, but I told Ty that you were my cousin," I stated.

"Oh really," he laughed, "So you pulled the old family card."

"Well it worked," I laughed.

A few minutes later I was squatting next the tub while Sam worked his hardening dick into my throat. The taste and feel of him in my jaws brought back memories of how we used to mess around after school. Sometimes we'd sneak into the locker room during gym and bust a quick nut together before anyone noticed we were missing. It was such a rush knowing that at any moment we could have gotten caught but thankfully we never did. Especially since we were both preacher's kids, that would have been the talk of the whole city. Not to mention how our parents would have laid hands on us with both anointing oil and the chastening rod. However, that was then and this is now, being together here we didn't have to worry about somebody finding out. We were free to fuck as much as we wanted to and this was one time I was gonna savor the moment. I grabbed a handful of each of Sam's ass cheeks and went for the goal. His grunts and moans turned me on even more as I closed my eyes and envisioned the last time we were together. The way he slowly massaged my walls with that thick pipe made me cream like crazy. As I continued to deep throat him, gagging a little each time he attempted to push it down to the balls, I wanted to feel him inside me. Yet knowing his temperament I decided not to pursue it. Then without even a glimmer of a warning the door flew open and there was Ty cupping his dick with one hand and a look of surprise and lust on his face I'll never forget. I didn't know how to react but just as I aimed to turn and say something Sam busted a fat but all over my face, neck, and shirt.

"Oh shit that was good as... FUCK where did he come from," Sam exclaimed, opening his eyes to realize we weren't alone anymore.

"Uh Devon, is this... I... I thought he was... I'll just talk to you after you clean up,"

18

Ty stammered as he collected his thoughts and left the room.

"I'm gonna assume that was Ty," Sam stated, before firing the shower up again.

Still speechless I just nodded and slowly rose to my feet. In my head I giggled a little because I'd just given this spill about not worrying about getting caught and then we get caught. Thankfully it was only Ty but that might not be such a good thing either considering the fact that he's my boss. Oh and let's not forget that my little ruse about us being cousins was now gone with the wind. I grabbed a face towel and washed the nut off me then proceeded to the office. When I got there Ty was laying across the sofa talking on the phone. From the tone in his voice it seemed to be a good conversation, but it was hard to tell with him sometimes.

"Devon, come sit down," Ty said, sitting up and motioning for me to sit next to him, "Well look my assistant just walked in with something I need to take care of now. I'll call you back when I leave the office," he

continued, rushing whoever he was talking to off the phone and turning his attention to me.

"Umm... you wanted to see me," I said nervously.

"Humm... yea I did, so you want to explain what I walked in on just now," he inquired glaring directly into my eyes.

"Well... I..."

"Look I get it, the cum splattering all over you said a lot. Still I think there's one detail that you may need to clear up. Sam isn't your cousin is he," he stated with a grin.

"No I'm not, but Devon and I have been friends since kindergarten, grew up in the same church, and experienced pretty much everything together," Sam interjected.

"Oh I see, and I must say that the pictures I was shown don't do you much justice. Still I'm not sure if you have what it takes to be the face of one of my events. Even though Devon and I will be there the responsibility of making sure that the guest

are happy is completely on you," Ty stated.

"Yea I gave him the rundown of what he has to do already," I said.

"Oh ok, and you think you can manage it sir?" Ty asked, carefully examining Sam's physique.

"I'm more than sure I can, as long as they don't get out of hand I'm good," Sam replied confidently.

"Humm ok... step over here son," Ty instructed, "I'm sure you know that there will be security at the event, and we have a 'no means no' policy since my assistant said he gave you the rundown of everything," he continued.

"Yea I expressed some concerns and he let me know all that. I still feel like somebody might try to test me but..."

"Don't worry about that, you as the host have the authority to ask them to leave and security as well as the rest of my staff and I will back you up. However, I don't need you *getting all crazy because somebody is a lil tipsy and they just rub up against you inadvertently. I mean given you're a sexy man and somebody is bound to be attracted to you, but just use your judgement and if you're really in an awkward position we'll handle it accordingly," Ty interrupted.*

"Ok, I just ain't trying to feel like I'm the buffet table at the Klump's family reunion," Sam laughed.

"I can assure that won't happen unless you allow it and by the way Devon, before I forget make sure that we have pads to protect the floor and Saturday morning I need the cleanup crew here ASAP. Also go ahead a get the paperwork ready for our friend here to sign and we can get him paid with no problems and reach me the measuring tape off the cabinet. Now umm... Sam... thank you Devon... would you mind dropping the towel so I can get some measurements on you," Ty stated, gently taking Sam by the hand and positioning him directly in front of him.

"Umm... measurements," Sam asked

confused by Ty's actions.

"Yes, I want to have you something made for Friday night and I need to be sure that the seamstress gets it right the first time," Ty explained.

"Uh Ty I don't know about that, I'm not trying to give anybody any more reason to molest me," Sam joked.

"I already had it on the agenda to take Sam shopping and the budget is already set," I chimed in from my desk.

"Ok, ok I'll fall back, but still go head and get an erection for me," Ty suggested, leaning back on the sofa.

"Umm... I thought you had got an eyeful earlier but ok," Sam agreed reluctantly as the towel fell to the floor.

"Just humor me son," Ty stated.

"Ok, I'm good," Sam replied, lubing his hand with spit and slowly attempting to stroke his dick to life.

"No need to be nervous man, just close your eyes and let it flow," Ty encouraged, noticing how tense Sam had gotten.

After a few minutes of stroking Sam finally got hard and Ty was more than impressed with what he saw. Especially those gorgeously plump cakes, but Sam wasn't feeling getting any attention back there. However, I was nowhere near ready for what happened next. Ty asked Sam if he could bust another nut but he didn't want him to jack off. Instead he wanted to watch him fuck me. Now I expected Sam to object but surprisingly he was more than willing to bend me over. I'll admit I was nervous but once Sam started eating my ass the inhibitions started to fade away. Ty just sat back and watched contently as the action unfolded. I wasn't sure if it was the money or maybe Sam had just changed a bit during our time apart, but whatever it was I had no qualms that Ty was getting his request and then some. It had been about a month or so since I'd had some dick but once Sam started to slide the head in I had no choice but to relax and allow him inside.

Initially it stung like hell, even though there was a considerable amount of lube used, Sam's dick was damn near thick as a beer can and nearly ten inches. Ty suggested that I lay on my back or ride it so I'd have more control, but it was still a fight.

Ten minutes later I was laying on my back with my legs pinned to my chest as Sam gently slid his pipe in and out of me. It still hurt a little but that euphoric sensation was quickly taking over as the fine line between pain and pleasure was erased. Gradually Sam began picking up speed and my hole got wetter and wetter with each stroke. I bit down on my bottom lip and clawed at Sam's back with one hand while the other clutched onto Ty's thigh. My deep, masculine voice filled the room as I cried out and grunted in ecstasy. For a second I contemplated sucking Ty's dick to quiet myself a little, but I figured it may be best not to cross that line. Ironically though he had been the last person to fuck me, but there's a story behind it trust me. However, I'm not gonna go into that right now and in that moment with Sam I didn't want him to know that anything had happened between us.

"Aww fuck this some good ass," Sam exclaimed, changing pace from steady deep strokes to pounding my guts.

"That shit look good too," Ty stated, with a mischievous smirk on his face, "You got a nice stroke game too," he added.

"It feels just as good as it looks if not better," Sam moaned.

"Ha, ha I'll leave that for Devon and whoever you may choose to smash at the party," Ty laughed.

"Doesn't hurt to try it just once," Sam countered with a smile.

"I could say the same for your phat cakes," Ty joked, playfully smacking Sam's ass.

"Ok, ok point taken," Sam said.

"Shit while yall niggas debating who's going to get fucked next I'm getting close and

Sam you already know what happens if I nut first," I interjected.

"True, I got you my dude," Sam conceded, slowing his stroke while I tried to clinch my ass muscles around his thick ass pipe.

"This some hot shit, and who knew your big masculine ass would have such a wet, creamy ass pussy," Ty hissed obviously getting turned on by the site of my asshole being milked, but knowing full well just how wet my ass could get.

"You know I really hate it when men refer to ass as pussy right," I growled disdainfully.

"Damn my bad, well I guess that's my que, you boys can finish up and I'm a get on out of the way," Ty said as he turned to leave.

"Ok boss, we'll see you later," Sam moaned, slowing down even more.

"Devon I put a list on your desk, make sure everything on it gets done and don't *forget to call the security company and inform then about every detail of how things are going to run Friday night. I don't want anybody to come up with no I didn't know bullshit," Ty instructed as he started to walk out the door, "I'd hate to fire anybody for having a good time on the job, but I certainly will. There's a time and place for everything," he continued.*

"Oh fuck... ok I'll... damn Sam... I'll handle it when we get... get done, aww shit nigga you in that shit," I moaned, struggling to put my words together and barely focusing on what Ty was saying.

"I'll make sure he gets it done," Sam chimed in.

"Give me that fucking dick son," I shrieked, grasping on to Sam's hips to pull him deeper.

"Damn... ok well I'm leaving now, yall go head and have your fun," Ty announced, closing the door behind him.

"Damn I was wondering when he was

going to leave so I could really enjoy this ass. That shit was kind of creepy bruh," Sam said, pretty much stopping mid-stroke and grinding his dick deeper inside me.

"I kind of figured you were only going along with it because he's the one who writes the checks," I laughed.

"Not really... well partially... but I honestly wanted to get in this ass when we were in the bathroom but I ain't know if you had prepped or not. I also went along with it because I wanted to see how much of a perv he would be or if he'd try to join in," Sam said, gently squeezing then smacking my ass before pulling his dick out.

"I didn't think he would have tried that, but he does definitely like to watch and sometimes direct a little," I replied.

"Yea I bet, but you go ahead and get started on that laundry list Ty left for you and then we can finish up what we started later on," Sam stated, leaning over and kissing me on the forehead.

"Fasho, why don't you go order the pizza so it can be on the way while you wait for me to finish all these calls and shit," I suggested, attempting to stand on legs that felt like noodles.

"Ok cool, my phone should be charged by now, so I'll go in the room and look up the number, plus I should probably also check in with moms to let her know I made it here safe," he said.

"Oh nah, it's a coupon on the fridge for Dominos, just use that, plus they owe me a free pizza because they fucked up my order last time. So make you mention that and get us some wings and a two liter too," I called behind him, "And yea calling Madam Nervine might be a good idea to because I'm sure she's already been blowing your phone up," I added.

"Watch it my nigga, and I see why you wanted to order out now," he joked, taking a glance in the fridge.

"Hey why not? If can save money and time I will bruh, and believe it or not the

fridge at my crib is pretty bare too," I laughed.

"True, and no I don't believe that, but I'll be in the room, you go ahead and get those calls and all that other shit Ty left for you done," Sam replied as he disappeared down the hall.

Even the innocent ones have a dark side...

Party

With

Me

PARTY WITH ME

Before my experience two years ago, I would have never imagined myself doing some of the things I did that week. In fact, if anybody would have told me I'd be involved in some crazy shit like that I would have laughed in their face. However, the reality now is that I did some things that I'm not exactly proud of but I did learn some things about myself. I'm also a lot more careful about who I allow to get close to me and more adamant about standing on my word. I think I'll just stick this little piece of food for thought in right here as well. If you know something is wrong don't do it, stay clear, do not pass go! It doesn't matter how much peer pressure there is or what people may think about you later. You are the one that has to live with the decisions that you make and you never want to put yourself in a position where you regret your own life. Ok, now that I've said that, we can get to what actually happened to me.

I had put a party ad on A4A, an online dating site and even though I canceled I'd been talking to this guy named Jayce, that was supposed to come, on and off for maybe two months on and off and I frankly thought he was full of shit. One thing that really made me weary of him was how he kept asking me to "party with T." I'll admit at that point I was a little wet behind the ears and I had no idea what that meant, so I asked. Then after he told me I was like hell no I'm not interested in this dude he can stop talking to me right now. However, he was very attractive, light-skin, thick, about 5'6, and beyond the partying shit, he seemed to be cool. So after two or three failed attempts at meeting I figured that we would never see each other face to face and maybe there wasn't any harm in continuing to chat. Now for those who may be reading this and wondering what the hell "T" is I'll enlighten you. T, Tina, or crystal is gay slang for methamphetamine, a recreational drug that does real crazy shit to your body and supposedly enhances the sex drive, but I'll get into more details about it later.

So one evening I'm sitting on my sofa watching TV and my phone rings. Earlier I had talked to another guy named Wayne on Jack'd about meeting up for drinks and I thought it may have been him, but I didn't recognize the number.

"Wassup, what you doing," an unfamiliar male voice chimed through the

phone.

"I'm chilling, but who is this," I replied.

"It's Jayce from A4A, you don't remember me," he asked.

"Not really," I answered, having an idea of who I was talking to but not completely sure.

"This is Partyguy248, remember we were supposed to meet at the freak party you were gonna have a couple months ago," he stated.

"Oh ok, what's up bruh," I said dryly.

"Nothing I'm on my way to New Orleans and I wanted to see you if that's cool with you." Jayce said.

"Uh yea I guess," I replied, figuring he was just bullshiting as usual.

"Ok so where do you want to meet," he asked.

"You can come here, I live alone," I answered, not really expecting anything from it.

"Cool well I'll be in the city in about thirty minutes, I'll call you back and get the address when I get closer," he stated.

"Ok, but I live on the west bank, I'm not in the city," I said.

"Ok I can come there unless you don't want me to," he replied, sensing the disinterest in my voice.

"Nah you good man, we can meet," I said, feeling a little remorse for my attitude.

"Aight, well I call you back when I get closer. You gon party with me tonight bruh?" he asked innocently.

"Man I already told you I ain't with that shit," I answered.

"So you don't want to see me now," he inquired dejectedly.

"Nah we can meet but I ain't fucking with no drugs bruh, I already told you that," I said sternly.

"Aight, aight, well I'll be that way in about twenty minutes, answer your phone bruh," he conceded

"Yea aight," I said, hanging up.

After I hung up the phone my mind started to race as I wondered if this dude was really coming. I mean if he was I definitely needed to get off my ass and take a shower. Plus, I needed to straighten up my apartment a little, hell I couldn't have company with dirty pots on the stove and dishes in the sink. Dude also had a fixation with eating ass so if he really did come I wanted to be certain that this hole was fresh and sweet for that tongue. However, even as the thoughts of what needed to be done meandered through my mind I just continued to sit there on my sofa watching TV and playing candy crush. Before I knew it twenty minutes has passed and there no call or text from Jayce. I was beginning to think that was going to be a no show as usual. So I proceeded to lounge and flip through channels till the phone rang a few minutes later, scaring the shit out of me.

"Hello," I answered dryly, recognizing the number from earlier.

"I'm almost on the west bank now, you still want to see me?" Jayce asked.

"Yea ok I'll text you the address now," I replied, still feeling like he wasn't really coming.

"Aight I got it, I should be there in about fifteen minutes," he stated.

"Ok," I said nonchalantly.

In my mind I was still thinking this dude is full of shit and he ain't coming. So I proceeded to just sit there and watch TV. Then no less than maybe ten minutes later my phone rings again. I notice it's the same number again so I pick up expecting an excuse or more time being added to the arrival.

"Hello," I answered.

"What's up I'm outside," Jayce said.

"Ok come on up, I'm upstairs in apartment ten, the only one with the light on," I replied as I flipped on my porch light.

"Aight, I'll be up in a sec," he said.

As I hung up the phone I was in shock that dude had really showed up. After all the bullshit he picked now to actually come through. However, I decided that I was going to be a good host and try to go with the flow. I looked out the window to see if anybody was really out there and sure enough there he was coming up the stairs. At that point my stomach sort of curled up in knots because I knew this dude was going to bring up that PnP shit again. Except for trying to smoke a blunt, I had never done drugs in my life and I wasn't about to start. After the second knock I went ahead and opened the door. Then in no less than maybe two minutes I was on my knees sucking his dick. He popped the question just as I had expected and I refused. I continued sucking his dick till it was almost hard and he stopped me saying he wanted get the T. Again he asked me to do it with him but I refused, till he offered me two hundred dollars to try it. I know it was a dumb decision but I agreed and we shot up and next thing I knew he was eating my ass. I didn't really feel any effects from the drug that I knew of but as things progressed I kept saying I needed to clean up. However, he didn't seem to care and just keep lapping at my hole like his life depended on it.

A few minutes later I still wasn't feeling anything, so I took another dose of the T. So before we resumed anything I went to my bedroom and got out my dildo. Jayce had attempted to put his dick in me but it wouldn't really get hard enough to stay in there. So I got my dildo and began to go to work while he watched. Little did I know that the drug was taking affect and my usual freakiness was about to get turned up a few notches. The site of me using the dildo must have excited him because next thing I knew the dildo had been replaced with his nine-inch dick. I normally don't bottom but while he was fucking me I sort of enjoyed it and started throwing this back at him. Then I got a text from the other guy, Donte, I'd talked to on Jack'd. Not thinking anything about it I casually asked him if he wanted to watch me get fucked. He agreed so I gave him the address and told him the door would be open. As Jayce continued to fuck me I started to get hornier. So next thing you know I have Jayce's dick and the dildo vibrating in my ass. It took a second to adjust to being stretched out a bit more but it felt good as fuck. Minutes later I get another text from Donte telling me he was on his way up. I replied with the apartment number and told him the door was unlocked just come inside.

"Damn you wasn't playing huh," Donte said as he entered my apartment.

"Nope but you why don't you take off some of those clothes and let me suck that dick while he fucks me," I replied.

"Nah I'm cool right now, let me just watch for a second," Donte stated as he sat

down on the sofa.

I'm sure you can imagine Donte sitting on the sideline didn't last for long and before I knew it I was getting plowed with ten and half inches of thick, hard, black dick. Surprisingly enough I was taking it with no problem and he was loving this ass. Jayce squatted down in front of me and I alternated eating his ass and sucking his dick while Donte fucked me good. By this point I was real horny and with every stroke of his dick I wanted more and more. I proceeded to talk shit to him demanding to be fucked harder and deeper. Jayce took a step back and watched for a second before jumping back in to get his dick sucked by Donte while he obliged me by fucking me hard and deep. I could feel my ass getting wetter by the second and the dick was feeling better the more he pounded me.

After about twenty minutes or so both Jayce and Donte had left but I was still feeling real antsy. I hadn't busted a nut and I was still horny as hell. So I hit up this dude I had been chilling with named Tre. I had met Tre one the same site I met Jayce on but at the time I was in a relationship and he was rebounding from one. However, we started hanging out and one thing led to another and somehow one night my dick slipped into his ass. Anyway, I hit him and explained what had been going down that night. He was a little upset with me for doing drugs, but ten minutes later I was on my way to pick him up. I felt a little jittery while I was on my way over there but I couldn't really focus on anything but sex. Thankfully the drive from my place to his wasn't that long plus it was the middle of the night so there wasn't any traffic. Went I got close by I called him so he could come down and meet me.

"I think you should drive back," I told him before sliding over to the passenger side.

"You sure you want me to drive yo shit," he questioned, knowing I'd never let anybody behind my wheel.

"Yea it's ok I'm right here and it's not that far," I replied.

"Ok..."

Once we were rolling again my moment of clarity was gone and my hormones took over again. Without any hesitation I had leaned over and popped his dick in my mouth, but before I could really get into it we were pulling up at my building. He aimed to get out of the truck but I held him down so I could get that dick hard and down my throat. Just as I was achieving my goal he suggested that we take it inside before anybody saw us. At that point I really didn't care but I knew he was right. After all, how would it look for me to get caught sucking dick in the parking lot when I had an empty apartment upstairs. So after a few more slurps I released him and we headed on upstairs. When we got inside there wasn't much talking other than him asking to shower and then instructing me while getting douched. After we we're both clean the toys came out and the fun began. Given I would never want to shot up again being with him was hot and fun. Too bad I had to be high for it to go down the way it did though.

For the next fifteen minutes or so Tre worked the dildo in my ass on high speed and the fleshlight on my dick while I alternated between sucking his dick and eating his ass. I knew getting inside me was something he'd been wanting to do for a while but I was always so adamant about being a top. Yet here I was tonight almost ready to receive the award for power bottom of the year and I had no qualms about it. once my hole was good and ready Tre threw my legs back and began rubbing his thick dick at my gate. Our eyes met momentarily in the darkness as he started to penetrate me. You would think after taking Donte's big beer can dick I would be open and ready for anything but I realized in that moment I had that real snapback shit. Jayce's dick felt good but half the time it wasn't completely hard because of the drugs, and Donte had literally fucked the shit out of me. I knew that wasn't a good look and I was definitely gon have to explain it to him later. Then just as my thoughts were coming together they scattered again as Tre went balls deep inside me. It hurt a little the first time but as he continued to fuck me the euphoria returned and I was soon begging to be fucked harder. Then in a daze of sporadic thought he lifted me off the bed and was fucking me in midair. Something I had done with him and a couple other dudes I had felt comfortable with, shit despite my 5'4, slim, toned frame I was pretty strong. Anyway he starts fucking me froggy style and soon we make our way out into my living room. I'm then laid on my back again on the arm of my raggedy ass sofa where we almost fall as he tries to really take advantage of topping me for a change. Then we move to my dining room table where he passionately massaged my wet hole with his moderately long and thick dick. Feeling a little adventurous I suggested that we take our party outside. Tre looked at me sort puzzled by the request for moment and then swept me up into his arms again. Standing at roughly six feet tall, and a pretty solid dude, it wasn't too much effort needed for him to pick me up.

When we got outside the cold night air quickly grabbed a hold of us but it only intensified the sensation as the endorphins ran amuck in my head. I clutched onto Tre's neck as he laid me back against the balcony wall and long stroked me good till I almost lost my grip. He then put me down and proceeded to hit it doggy style. I closed my eyes for a brief second before reason came to whisper in my ear again. Reminding me that we were outside on the balcony and at any moment a car could pass or pull up or somebody could come out of their apartment and catch us. Yet I just dismissed my cautionary feelings and tried to focus on watching the street and being aware of what was going on around me. However, the deeper and harder Tre pounded me the harder it was to focus on anything. My ass was super wet and there was a lusty hunger that had been unleashed in me that I'd never seen before. Maybe there was a lesson to be learned in this experience, but I knew one thing for sure I was horny as fuck and it seemed like I couldn't get enough. Then just as I was falling back into a trance a set of headlights sent us retreating back into my apartment. Once back in my room I peered out of the window watching as the headlights turned into a dark colored SUV, driven by this sexy bald headed guy, and pulled into the driveway next door. Part of me wanted to go back out and fuck in front of them and maybe even ask him to join, but my mind settled with getting fucked by my homie in every position possible.

After what may have been another hour of fucking we tried going outside again. This time I tried my hand at riding his dick but once again we were chased inside by a pair of headlights coming up the street. So we went back to the bed and as Tre worked my hole I began to notice that something was wrong. I'd been stroking and getting dicked down this whole night but I was still nowhere near a nut. Then on top of that my dick wouldn't stay hard. Tre had already implanted two nuts deep in my guts but I still wasn't satisfied. I wanted to bust a nut too but no matter how I tried I couldn't bring myself to a climax. Eventually Tre fell asleep on me and I was left up alone still horny and craving a nut. I grabbed the dildo turned it on high and jammed it all the way inside me while I worked the fleshlight on my dick. The feeling of both being pleasured at the same time was amazing but my dick still wasn't working and I was getting nowhere.

"Dude you might as well give it up till that shit runs out of your system," Tre said groggily, noticing that I was still up and at it.

"I'm almost there I can feel it, but my dick just won't stay hard," I groaned.

"It's not going to nigga you need to take yo ass to sleep," he scolded.

Realizing he was probably right I began to get a little worried about what I had allowed to happen and the effects it was having on me. Still I was laying there but ass naked and horny as fuck. Tre had gone back to sleep and I was too juiced to even think about sleeping. In those few moments of clarity though, I knew one thing was certain, I would never do this shit again. Then just as I was about to give up my phone rings in the other room. I hop up to grab it and I notice a shadow outside my window. Hesitantly I exam the figure as I retrieve the phone and notice it was Jayce calling to tell me he was outside.

By this point it was almost five am and my high was slowly coming down so my voice of reason was a little bit stronger. I thought about what I had allowed to transpire and was weary of letting this dude back into my house. Especially with my homeboy sleeping in the other room, I didn't know what other kind of shit this dude might come up with and I had to protect my friend. However, my hormones got the best of me and I opened the door instead of sending back to wherever he had been for last few hours. Yet with a little bit of cognizance gained I made up in my mind to keep him away from my boy. For the most part I did a pretty good job till we started fucking again and this time Jayce's dick seemed to work a little better but I realized his stroke game was shit. So then maybe an hour or so later here comes Tre all glassy-eyed and still half asleep. Jayce's eyes lit up when he saw him and I was almost relieved that he was awake but still not so sure about the two interacting. Truth was I'd grown some deep emotions for Tre and having him there with me that night sort of fortified them. Anyway that's another tale for another day. So I'm lying on my back with Jayce attempting to fuck me and I'm getting a little aggravated with his lack of skill. So I tell Tre to come kneel beside me so I could suck his dick. Once I had him hard again I basically pushed Jayce off me and let Tre fuck deep till I couldn't take anymore. Then to add more drama to an already crazy night, which had now spilled into the next day there's another knock on my door. I quickly jump up and whisk Jayce and Tre into my room while I grab something to put on. Then I open the door to see my mom.

"Good morning," she chirped, "you ready to take me to the store," she continued.

"Ummm... no I forgot... I have company I'll call you when I'm ready," I stammered, flustered and mortified at the same time.

"Oh umm ok..." she replied as I pretty much turned her away without thinking.

Now I knew I was going to hear about that later and I sort of felt bad about it but shit I had company. Not that it made the situation any better but I damn sure wasn't about to tell her what happened and I definitely wasn't leaving anybody in my house. I trusted Tre but I didn't trust Tre being alone with Jayce. So what else could I do? Then just as I had suspected I get back into my bedroom and find Jayce trying to get up on Tre. Unfortunately, but fortunate for me, his dick wouldn't get hard and Tre was just as unimpressed with him as I was and other than eating his ass he wasn't getting anywhere with Tre. So noticing that I was now back in the room the failed attempt at fucking my homeboy was ended and I stated the obvious.

"Tre what time you got to be at work," I asked, conveniently interrupting them.

"Like ten," Tre replied.

"Ok well it's almost nine now, so we should probably get moving," I suggested.

"Damn do you have to go now," Jayce whined, "I really want to see how that ass feels on the inside," he added.

"You've felt enough," Tre snapped abruptly, pretty much pushing Jayce off as he stood up.

"And I have some errands to run too," I added.

"Well what if I took you to work," Jayce inquired, still desperately trying to get in some kind of way.

"Nah I'm good, my boy got me," Tre answered dryly.

"Aight well I guess I'll get at you later then bruh," Jayce said, realizing that the party here was officially over.

"Yea just text me later and we'll see what's up," I stated.

So Jayce left and Tre and I showered and got ready to start our day. I couldn't believe what had happened over the last twelve hours, but at that point I couldn't take any of it back so it was no use in sulking over it. However, I did know that I would never let anybody talk me into doing some stupid ass shit like that again. Even though the night did have its highlights I would definitely have to pass on seeing a replay. Tre scolded me again for my actions, but also concurred to fact that some hot shit had went down that night. Especially since he got to see and feel a side of me he'd never experienced before and likewise with me. So again I'll reiterate what I stated in the beginning. If you know for a fact that something just doesn't feel right or you're not into whatever may be presented to you, stick to your guns. Don't let anybody pressure you into doing anything that you know you will regret later. Better yet, if it will *hurt you or endanger your life, don't take that risk, especially with a complete stranger. Hell it was definitely a lesson well learned for me and the next time somebody ask me to "party" I'll just pass and keep it moving. That night brought some things out of me that I never knew was there and will probably never mention, yes I left some shit out, sorry. Plus, letting some random guy you meet online inject you with some shit you know nothing about is fucking stupid as hell and may not end well. I was fortunate enough to survive the ordeal with some repercussions but yet I'm still here to tell about it while there are others you weren't so lucky. Yes, I did some research on that shit after the fact and what I found only makes me more adamant about not doing it again. Shit can really fuck you up, not to mention the shakes, vomiting, diarrhea, and cold sweats I had the day after. Oh and it took about two days before I could get my dick to get hard again. Plus, I had to hide all that shit from my mom and act like I was just too busy to do anything else till all the symptoms had passed. So with all that trust me I won't be walking that road again. yall be cool and be safe and if anybody ask you to "party" with them make sure you know what's up before you do.*

Discovering Me

*Looking out of the mirror there's the image of a broken man
The reflection of a man that's too afraid to show his insecurities
A man living in his own shadow
There is a man troubled by his own truth
Ashamed of mistakes he has made but yearning to find purpose
in passion*

*Looking out of the mirror is a man that's been hurt, neglected,
and abused
A man whose heart is heavily guarded
He keeps his emotions locked inside with fear of being a fool
Past experiences have paralyzed his spirit
Inhibiting his ability to love without the boundaries of
yesterday's pain*

*Looking out of the mirror is a man that must find strength in his
own eyes
He knows the courage to move on must come from within
The man in mirror realizes that the fate of those around him rest
on his shoulders
Knowing failure isn't an option he pushes himself forward
Casting aside his own fears is his greatest test*

*In the mirror is the reflection of man refined by the flames of
trial and struggle
Standing there is the unique signature of individuality that only
God can see
In the mirror is a man that's triumphed and failed but never gave
in
In the mirror I can see myself
A man who has persevered to rise from the ashes and accept all
his flaws with grace and wisdom*

Take A

Load Off

Every hard working man deserves a break...

TAKE A LOAD OFF

If walls could talk I wonder what stories they would tell. Between my office, my bedroom, and the suite at the loft I'm not sure I would want to know what they have to say. Yet I'm sure between all of them they could probably write a whole book about my ass and the shit I do behind closed doors. I mean being the owner of an adult entertainment company there aren't too many taboo things that could happen right? However, some people may think that my methods are a bit eccentric or perverse. Yes, it's true I fuck some of my models to test drive their skills. If it's a top that's auditioning I may have them bring a partner or pair them up with somebody and of course I watch to make sure that nigga stroke game is on point. Still this is adult entertainment who doesn't dip into the cookie every now and then. I'm sure I'm not the only one, but with me there's never any feelings involved. It's all business and my guys know it. Now I may have an addiction to voyeurism and other fetishes I may need to control but again this is porn. Anyway I'm not going to sit here and try to defend the way I run my business. My movies do well, my books sell, my parties are always hot, and my employees can vouch that we have no financial problems so I'm good.

Well anyway, my assistant and I have been planning an event for Friday night and it has been hectic. More so for me though since I've delegated most of the planning to Devon, my assistant. He's actually pretty efficient but I'm still a little nervous about how it's all going to come together. However, if he's going to be my protégé I have to give him room to spread his wings at some point right? So right now I'm laying here in my king-sized bed alone and feeling some kind of way. I thought about calling one of my regulars but I really didn't feel like dealing with anybody trying to stay over or getting in their feelings because I busted my nut and was ready to call it a night. I browsed through my phone and found an old video of myself fucking this thick, sexy lil redbone nigga named Tristian. Those gorgeous cakes jiggle like jelly as I pounded that creamy, wet hole that was gripping my dick like a glove. I thought he had mad potential to get in the biz but he was a PK and didn't want to be on camera. I snuck this little footage one night while he had his face buried in the pillow. Too bad he was killed in an accident about a year ago because he would have been perfect to call right now. He'd let me bust in that mouth then fuck that ass till we both came, clean up, and bounce.

After watching a few more vids in my phone my dick was throbbing and begging to be released. I really didn't want to jack off but what other option did I have since I didn't want to be bothered another nigga and a chick was definitely out of the question. My flesh light was worn out and I was too tired to drive to the Den or ZA. Not to mention I didn't want to pay the covers. Even though I was cool with both the owners and they probably would have let me in free I'd rather support my colleagues. So again here I am laying in this bed with a hard dick watching homemade phone cam porn. Then as I continued to browse through I came across a few clips from the night I got my first taste of my assistant Devon's sweet hole. There was one of him giving me head, a POV shot of me fucking those smooth chocolate cakes doggy style, and another one of him riding my dick. Watching those vids reminded me of how I'd caught him sucking this dude named Sam's dick in the bathroom. He claimed that dude was his cousin but I knew that was some bullshit, especially after I saw that. Then it got even hotter when Sam came out the bathroom and I suggested that they give me a little show. I didn't really expect them to go along with it, but I guess if you get caught up like they did and think your job might be on the line you'd do anything. Sam fucked Devon like he was fresh off the prison bus and Devon's hungry hole swallowed that long, thick dick like a toy. When I first met Devon I never would have though such a big masculine guy could be that much of a power bottom. He's 6ft tall and roughly about 220lbs with a perfectly chiseled body wrapped in the smoothest chocolate skin I've ever seen. Sam was a work of art as well, standing around 5'11" and pure muscle with a gorgeous ass that giggled with every thrust as he pounded

Devon's guts.

I laid there for about five minutes replaying the scene in my head. My dick throbbing and leaking inside my boxers as I gently caressed my torso. Squeezing my pecs and pinching my nipples while my imagination twisted reality into fantasy. The visual set fire to my hormones and as hard I tried to resist the urge to milk my rock I couldn't help it anymore. So I slid out of my boxers and grabbed my lube and toys out of the nightstand. Then just as I finished lubing up my bullet, flipped it on and got it in place my phone rang. Seeing that it was only Devon I ignored it and proceeded with what I was doing. I slowly slid the two-inch piece of vibrating metal into my hole and braced myself as I kicked the speed up. Then I popped the top off of my fleshlight and prepped it for penetration. By now my dick was throbbing and moans coming from the video on my phone only stirred my hormones more. It might sound a little conceded but my homemade porn kind of turns me on more than the professional shit out there. Even the pro/am stuff I was in when I was younger. Not to mention it love to see a pair of phat, juicy cakes milking my dick. so I closed my eyes and let the sex serenade me as I slowly glided the fleshlight up and down my shaft. Feeling it grip and suck my shit into those soft, moist walls with each stroke. Then just as I was really getting into it my phone rang again.

"Aww fuck," I exclaimed as I swiped my finger across the screen to answer it.

"Hey daddy," the voice of my four-year-old god daughter chirped through the speaker.

"What's going on cupcake," I replied, quickly flipping off the toy.

"Mommy said you were coming to see us Sunday, is that true? Are you going to bring me something when you come? Will you let me ride on your bike?" she interrogated, not even giving me a chance to answer one question before she asked another.

"Yea baby girl I'm coming but I'm not bringing the bike because I heard it was

supposed rain out there Sunday evening," I answered.

"Aww well can we go see the horsies by Mama Tee's house," she whined in disappointment.

"Well see and maybe if you're a good girl for the rest of the week I'll bring you a little surprise," I stated, laughing to myself at how relentless and spoiled she'd gotten, though it was mostly my fault.

"Oh I promise daddy, I'll be really, really good for mommy," she chimed excitedly.

"Ok now let me talk to your mommy and you go get ready for bed aight," I said.

"Ok, here she is," she sang as I heard her handing the phone off.

"Hello... Ty I'm sorry... I didn't even know she had my phone," Mimi began to stammer.

"No worries ma, how's it going?" I inquired.

"It's going pretty good," she replied slowly.

"Uh oh, I don't like the sound of that, what's wrong Mimi," I asked, knowing that she was trying to either cover something up or ask me for money.

"It's nothing for real, I'm just tired, Lai is a handful these days and them people worked the shit out of me at my job today," she answered.

"Ok so everything is good huh," I said in disbelief.

"Yes Ty we're good, there's no bills due or anything going on you need to know about ok," she replied, sensing my suspicions.

"Ok, ok I'll take your word for it," I said.

"Thank you, but this pussy is dry as fuck with nobody to lick it," she blurted out catching me off guard.

"Well damn ok, as horny as I am right now I might have to jump on a red eye and do *that for you," I laughed.*

"Boy stop playing you too busy licking boy pussy to worry about mine," she stated with an air of jealousy.

"Sounds like you feeling some kind of way about that," I laughed.

"I mean shit, you used to do more than for me when you were here, not I can't even get a dick pic from yo ass," she pouted.

"Damn ma I ain't know you was missing this dick like that," I said.

"Whatever you Mr. Gay Porn Producer now you ain't got time for the pussy no more," she continued.

"Ok come on now, do you hear yourself? That sounds crazy as fuck ma," I replied, a little annoyed by her last comment.

"I bet if all them ATL niggas and fans you got knew you like a lil pussy every now and then you wouldn't be so popular," she proceeded, knowing she was pressing my buttons now.

"Aight you losing it now, but I got something for you when I see you," I warned.

"What you gon do nigga? You ain't gon whip my ass and you damn sure ain't gon fuck me," she taunted.

"That's what you want though ain't it," I stated, "I mean you talking all that shit instead of just saying Ty I want you to fuck me when you come out here. I guess that's just too easy though right? You can't just ask for what you want you got to start some bullshit before we can get to the real shit right? You can't just say it can you? Oh and since we talking about fuckin what happened to that mandingo warrior nigga with the hurricane tongue that you told me about," I retorted.

"You know what Ty I can't fuck with you and that nigga was crazy as hell so fuck that shit baby," Mimi exclaimed.

"He was crazy how," I asked.

"That nigga started getting all possessive and shit ain't nobody ever told his as I was his girl. He fucked me real good so *we would chill but that was it. So when that nigga started talking about how this pussy was his and I'm a be for him forever he had to go. Nigga get the fuck out my bed with that weird ass shit, lose my number please, and don't worry about seeing me no more," she answered.*

"That pussy was his as long as his dick was in it huh," I joked.

"You damn right nigga... wait a minute you tried that shit nigga, but anyway let me get off this phone and I'll talk to you later or see you this weekend. Whichever should happen to come first," she snapped back.

"Aight I'll get with you before I come ma and kiss Lai goodnight for me," I said, still laughing to myself.

"Ok bye Mr. Stingy," she said.

"Man cut that out ma, you'll be calling me something else when I get there," I laughed.

"Boy bye whatever, I can tell how you

just laughed you don't want no pussy," she retorted sassily.

Girl bye, we'll see," I stated before hanging up.

At that point my horniness had all but passed but I was still laying there with a greasy dick and a toy in my ass. So I started to go back to what I was doing then I remembered Devon had tried to call me. I looked at the clock on my dresser and saw that it was almost eleven and I definitely needed to get some sleep so I could be alert for the meetings I had the next morning. So I picked up my phone and listened to the voicemail Devon left and then debated if I should go head and call him back. I had done a pretty good job teaching him the ropes but there were still some decisions and calls that only I could make. That's the price of being the boss right? Anyway I opted to just send him a text telling him to go ahead with the email blast for our VIP members and setup the social media ad to run for the next two days. I knew that he was nowhere near ready to go public with the event but maybe a little pressure was what he needed to help him tie up the rest of those loose ends. This was the first time I'd let somebody else take the reins and I knew he knew that his job was on the line. However, at the same time I knew he had what it took to pull everything together, I just hated that he procrastinated so much. Devon was smart and sharp but easily distracted sometimes. Plus, I'm still shocked he lied to me about Sam but Sam seemed surprised too so maybe Devon did have a plan, he was taking risk but I guess it'll work out. Tomorrow we are supposed to interview strippers and with our host in place the guys had to be on point to compare. Still setting up the interviews was Devon's job so I had no idea who was coming. I did have a contingency plan in place just case something fell through the cracks. I wasn't going to allow my reputation to be marred or any fans or guests to be disappointed. There is one other little detail I didn't mention to Devon and planned to keep it to myself. The VIP room that I was setting up would also be wired to live feed showing in the main space and all the hot shit that would go down that night would be recorded. I figured Devon might have been in too deep if I had left that to him so my hands were still in it anyway.

After about ten or fifteen minutes of lying there and just letting my mind run wild I decided I would go head and jack my dick, shower, and then call it a night. That conversation with Mimi kind of killed my mood a little bit but it didn't change the fact that I hadn't busted a nut in a minute. I didn't want to jack off because I wanted to save all my nut for the party Friday night. Usually I don't get involved in the action but since we had a host and extra security at this one I could afford to play a little. At the last event we had there was this slim, chocolate lil muthafucka that was sexy as hell and I wanted a piece of that so bad but I couldn't get it. Devon was at the bar and my other assistant was working on a nut and his last paycheck as he rode the stripper's dick. So that left me to oversee everything and even though I had security there I still had to keep tabs on how shit was going down. Then on top of that I spotted one of the guards ducked off in a corner with one nigga sucking his dick while the other one lapped at his balls and ass. Now of course I prescreened these guys to make sure they would be comfortable in that kind of environment. Nevertheless, they all knew the rules so after I watched him take a lil dick and get his nut I kindly pulled him aside, informed him that he was fired, and had his coworker escort him out. People may think I'm an asshole sometimes but even I abide by the rules so hey it is what it is right, right. So anyway I wanted that lil slim piece of chocolate last time but couldn't get to him. This time I made sure his name was on the VIP list and he wasn't leaving the loft till I had a taste of that ass. I know, I know I just finished talking about firing somebody for fucking while working but listen to me good. Right above that I said there would be extra security this time and I had a host to take care of the guest. Plus, I am the boss and besides that it's only in the VIP room so nobody would see me. Yep I'm funny like that, wouldn't be me if it was any other way.

So anyway, after the text conversation

was over I just laid there with my thoughts meandering through fantasyland. It wasn't long before my dick started to throb with the anticipation of being pleasured and I allowed myself every privilege of giving it what it deserved. The video on my phone sang tantalizing arias of lust and sensuality. So I fired the bullet back up and slowly let my dick invade the walls of the fleshlight. For a toy it was surprisingly realistic and the warm, moist skin felt surely close to the real thing. I closed my eyes and gently began grinding my hips around. Forcing my thick eight and half inch dick deeper into the fleshlight and maximizing the intensity of the bullet. I began to breathe deep and bite down on my bottom lip trying my hardest to muffle my moans. Yet with each stroke it felt better and better. My asshole was wet and I could feel my dick pre-cumming like crazy inside my handheld love tunnel. The walls in this condo weren't the thickest and occasionally I'd heard my neighbors' conversations or their own sexual escapades. Which I actually thought was hot till I saw the neighbor. Body was on point but her face was jacked up and when she opened her mouth it got even worst. Can you imagine a female version of the rapper Flavor Flav with Kim Kardashian's or Beyoncé's body, and a busted grill? If you can catch that visual, that's her you see right there, but the guys I saw her with were all A-list type dudes. Guess she was either just an easy fuck, had some good pussy or head, or the dudes were just desperate and needed a nut. Shit I've even been tempted to knock on that door a couple times. However, I knew for sure she knew I fucked men, but from the way she looks at me sometimes I think she might still let me smash if I really wanted.

Twenty minutes later I had lost complete control and I couldn't hold back any longer. Then hearing myself and Devon on the video only turned me on more. I caught myself responding and talking shit to it a few times. Then the images of Sam plowing that ass with those juicy cakes of his jiggling with each thrust flooded my mind. I wanted to taste that sweet looking hole so bad my mouth was watering. The playful banter we had, had was kind of hot too but I knew the only way either

of us was getting fucked would be in a fantasy.
I had only really given up the ass a few times
and only really enjoyed it maybe once or
twice. However, I do love to get my ass ate
and I ain't never been shy about sucking dick
either. Shit that nigga Sam could definitely
taste these cakes, hell I might try to pull his
ass into that VIP room Friday night. I mean
once he sees who else is there I'm sure he
won't mind participating and that extra check
for the video footage might sway him a bit too.
Maybe I'd get the chance to get him and that
lil sexy chocolate muthafucka to link up and
do some hot shit for the camera. "Damn that
would be hot," I remember thinking to myself
as I plotted how I'd bring together the hottest
amateurs I knew and some of black gay porn's
elite stars.

As I wrapped my mind around a plan I
could almost see it all unfolding right in front
of me. Thoughts that made my dick throb even
more as I continued caress it with the tight
warm walls of the fleshlight. I licked my lips
and grunted loudly while my hormones
orchestrated their own scene with me as the

star. In the mirror on my closet door I caught a glimpse of myself giving my pipe the best workover ever. It glistened with lube and precum that dripped down my balls as rocked my hips. The volume of my moans increased steadily but I no longer cared if anybody was listening. In fact, I kind of wanted the attention. The thought of my neighbors trying to piece together the mystery of what I was doing and who I was doing it with only added fuel to the fire as I pressed my way towards a bursting climax. A flood was imminent and I was desperate with anticipation. I kicked the speed all the way up on the bullet and tossed the fleshlight aside. I was getting closer to an explosion with every stroke and the thought of my hot juice splattering over my body drove me wild. For some men the thought of cum on them was disgusting, even if it is their own, but the satisfaction of spraying myself down with my own pleasure gave me another level of ecstasy. Call me nasty, call me a freak, call me whatever but it won't stop me from doing me. That nut was about to shoot all over my stomach, chest, face, and with any luck I might even get some in my mouth. The feelings of lust and bliss intensified with each passing moment. My subtle moans escalated to vociferous grunts as I felt my load coming to a peak. "Aww fuck nigga," I shouted, feeling my balls tighten, letting me know I was getting close to the goal.

Five minutes later I was laying there with cum all over my chest, stomach, thighs, and there was even some dripping down my left cheek. This had to be one of the best nuts I had gotten in a long time and I loved every minute of it. I stuck my tongue out as far as I could get it and attempted to lick off the cum that was dripping down my face. That didn't work too well so I just used my hand to guide it onto my lips. Yes, I'm a real nasty nigga and if you ever fucked with me you'd see more than that. My nut was sweet as usual so there were no worries there. No bitter aftertaste from this juice. I ate a good diet and keep myself healthy so sweet tasting nut was the result. Trust me it works and all my partners can testify lol. I was still feeling a little high from the experience and the bullet was actually still going strong, but I knew I had to make a move soon. I mean it was nobody there but me but once my hormones settled I wasn't going to want to roll over in no cum. So I clicked off the bullet and forced myself to get up. I grabbed the remote from the nightstand and started the shower. Technology was amazing yall and being able to start my shower and shit from the bed was a convenience I had to had when I saw it.

A few minutes later, after gathering myself and making sure there was no cum on my sheets, I stepped into the shower and allowed the water to massage my whole body. Today had been a long fucking day and that nut I just got plus these body jets was a nice way to end this crazy ass day. Only problem was I had to get tomorrow and do all this shit over. Then again, tomorrow might not be so bad, I was going to be doing interviews, well more like auditions, for strippers. There were a few other meetings scheduled but I could definitely have some fun with those interviews. So anyway this was definitely a nice end to a busy day and a load off me. Now I can take my happy ass back in this bed and sleep real good till the alarm clock starts screaming at me. The life of a boss ain't easy, but it definitely has it rewards.

Ty Eros

Stress Relief

It's been a long hard day
Call, meetings, mountains of paperwork
Days like this I wish I had a 9-5
Even when I think I'm done it's still more to do
But that's the cost of being the boss
No social life, no love life, no sex
What did I get myself into
What's funny is I'm the CEO of a porn company
So everything around me is SEX, SEX, SEX
Ok I won't lie I do get some but when it's in your face all
day you can't help but want more
My dick throbs all day
Begging to be freed from its captivity
Yearning to be pleasured
In desperate need of a release
I sit here and contemplate how good a nut would feel after a
stressful day
Think about my warm hands gently caressing my hard
dick to a creamy climax
Shooting hot cum all over myself
Letting it drip down my body as my mind calms
The tension and anxiety of my day fade into distant
memories
I shower and wash away the residue of my licentious
indulgence
Finally, peace comes cradled in sweet slumber before I rise to
do it all again

MAKE IT HOT

It was one of those days I'd never forget. September 19, 2013 was the day I had one of the best freak sessions of my life. However, I think I was more surprised by who was involved rather than what actually happened. I can remember waking up around ten or eleven that morning and starting my normal routine. I got out of bed, took a piss, washed my hands, brushed my teeth, and showered, but since I had the day off I hopped back in the bed. Then just as I was dosing back off to sleep my phone rang.

"What's up boo?" Kayla's voice shrieked through my phone before I could really answer it.

"Nothing much ma, I'm just chillin at the crib, what's good with you?" I responded.

"Trying to see what's up with that dick papi," she announced, yes she's straightforward bout hers.

"It all depends on what you want to be up with it," I laughed, just as a message alert rang on my iPad, putting somewhat of a stake in the thick sexual tension that was building in the conversation, "but hold on a minute ma," I

continued, taking a second to check the message.

"Yeah aight, but that better not be no bitch trying to get to that dick," she responded menacingly.

"Man calm down ma, ain't even no shit like that going down around this piece," I answered coldly, "It's just Big anyway," I added.

"He can't get no dick either," Kayla laughed, entertained by her own sick humor.

I remained silent as I read the message asking what I had up for the day. I quickly replied explaining what was up, so I wouldn't keep Kayla waiting too long. I also took the precaution of putting my iPad on silent so there wouldn't be any further suspicions. Even though a nigga was fucking other bitches she didn't need to know that. Hell she might be a lil off, but the bitch did give some fire ass head and she had some bomb ass pussy.

"Raheim!" Kayla barked impatiently.

"Damn girl hold up," I replied.

"What lame bitch is that you got texting you nigga," she retorted.

"Man I already told you that was my nigga trying to see what I'm doing. You need to stop being so damn paranoid ma. You know you the only one getting this dick," I said smoothly lying through my teeth.

"Humm... you'll tell me anything to get this pussy huh nigga," Kayla stated dryly.

"Damn ma why it got to be like that?" I asked, trying not to laugh.

"Don't play innocent nigga, I know all about you and that bitch Keisha fucking last week," she barked.

"And I bet she the one that told you that shit right," I asked.

"No my roommate Lisa and that bitch was talking about it the other day and I just happened to walk in on the conversation so she confessed," Kayla said, "and how would she know about the tat on your thigh if you ain't fucking her nigga," she continued.

"So I guess I'm supposed to be fucking Lisa too right," I mocked, "Since they just causally having conversations about me when they know you in the house listening."

"You might be nigga, and you still

didn't answer my question," she yelled.

"Come on now, you know that hoe Lisa been feeding you bullshit since the first time you told her about us fucking. So bam there it is you told her we fucked and how we fucked, so she obviously wants to try it for herself. I mean shit... I know I ain't the best looking muthafuckin nigga around this bitch but shit... the bitch always talking shit trying to separate you from yo dick supply. Now to answer your question, I do dance from time to time for a lil extra change and I have seen both them hoes at the club," I stated, covering my ass.

"Humm...you might not be but you far from ugly though, so maybe you're right about them bitches. Humm, I don't blame that bitch for wanting to get a piece of yo ass, but you ain't deny fucking Keisha either, however I better not ever catch her or any other bitch on that dick," Kayla said.

"Why would I let her ass catch me with some other bitch," I said to myself, knowing her ass is a fucking lunatic, "You know it ain't like that ma," I replied.

"Yeah, so what's up then," she pressed.

"I don't know you tell me baby girl," I

answered, bouncing the ball back in her court.

"Nigga you know how mama likes it," she laughed.

"True and you know how daddy likes to serve it," I laughed, just as I got another text from Big.

"Yo, you say she a freak right? So what up with letting yo boy come run through that shit too nigga?" the text read.

I paused for a minute and chuckled under my breath, careful not give that crazy bitch Kayla any incentive to think anything was up. Even though I was now scheming about how to get her to let Big fuck her too. I told him she might go for it, but I wasn't sure and would hit him back.

"Yo ma, you ever thought about doing a threesome?" I blurted out quickly before I had a chance to change my mind.

"Nigga what the fuck? How you just gonna ask me some shit like that out the fucking blue? You ain't about to get me in the bed with no other bitch. I'll cut both of you muthafuckas," she snapped back bitterly.

"Nah, nah, nah ma, it ain't even like that. I'm talking about you, me, and my homeboy," I announced, not believing what I was saying myself.

"Nigga what? You saying you'd let another nigga beat this good ass pussy up right in front yo face," she asked jokingly.

"Yeah, if you down, but I ain't just gon stand on the sideline, I'm fucking too."

"How the fuck two niggas gonna fuck my pussy at the same time," she asked.

"Shit it's possible, or one can get in that sweet pussy while the other one gets up in that ass, or in your mouth," I said.

"Sound like we might need three niggas for that shit to happen then huh," she laughed.

"I knew yo ass was freak," I replied.

"I know you did, why else would you be fucking me," she snapped back.

"Ha, ha, you kind of got a point on that note ma. So are you coming over or what," I asked, cutting to the chase.

"Hell yeah nigga, but who this other

nigga supposed to be though?"

"Damn, so you really bout doing it huh," I questioned in surprise.

"I asked didn't I?"

"Fasho, it's my nigga Big," I replied.

"Is the name any indication of what he's packing," she asked.

"Fuck I don't know, peeps been calling that nigga Big or big boy since I met him. Shit I ain't never seen that nigga's dick," I snapped.

"Did I say you did nigga, calm yo ass down, shit why niggas act like that? Fuck I done seen my girl's pussies before and I ain't tripping," Kayla replied.

"So have I," I thought to myself, "I ain't tripping either, but that's just something I don't know. So what time are you coming over," I asked.

"Shit nigga I'm about to be in yo driveway in a minute," she answered.

"Oh damn, aight let me get some shit to put on," I said, jumping up off the bed.

"For what?" she asked.

"I can't walk outside naked," I laughed.

"You ain't got to come outside nigga, just come unlock the door because I'm here," Kayla said, simultaneously setting her car alarm to announce her arrival.

"Aight," I said, grabbing my iPad and walking to the front door to meet her.

Before I walked out of the bedroom I texted Big and told him we were good. He texted me back a few seconds later and told me that he's be over soon as he ate and showered. I warned him not to take too long, tossed the iPad back on the bed, and proceeded down the steps and just as I reached the bottom Kayla was banging on the door. "Hold on I'm coming," I yelled as I approached the door. I could see Kayla's thick, sexy figure through the window and my dick instantly started to stiffen up.

"Damn nigga what took you so long? You was in there playing with yo dick or something?" she wailed as I opened the door to let her in.

"Nah ma I got you here for that."

"Oh really," she said as she grabbed hold of my semi-hard manhood, "Aww damn, I really miss this shit baby," she continued as she proceeded kiss my neck and work her way down my body with her tongue.

"Damn girl, I ain't going nowhere, slow down," I said while grabbing on to her shoulders as she viciously gulped down my dick. Sucking as if it was the last one she'd ever see. Noticing that she was paying me no mind I said fuck it and just went with the flow. I began to roughly fuck her face, forcing my fat, 9in dick all the way down her throat. Grasping tightly to my thick ass cheeks she didn't miss a beat, working her lips on that shit as if she was a fucking professional. I reached down and picked her up by her waist simultaneously causing her skirt to fall in the other direction exposing her naked ass. "Damn this bitch really is a freak," I thought to myself, "but fuck it, so am I," I laughed to myself as I plunged tongue first into that pretty, clean-shaven, caramel pussy.

After about five minutes of this I managed to walk back us up to my bedroom never missing a beat in our vertical 69. I knew by now the blood was probably rushing to her head and I definitely wasn't trying to kill her.

Not yet that is, but once the dick gets up in her pussy, who knows.

"Oh damn baby, you got a fiya ass tongue," she said, wildly bucking her ass back and forth.

"Yeah nigga eat that pussy," I heard a familiar masculine voice whisper in my ear, "Lick that ass too nigga! Get it good and wet so my dick don't have no problems getting in that shit," he continued.

Finally, I recognized the voice and reluctantly looked up to see Big standing on the side of the bed stroking his dick. "Am I too late," he said aloud, announcing his presence. Kayla looked back, licked her lips, and went back to sucking my dick. He climbed on the bed and stooped down beside me. He then grabbed a handful of Kayla's fat ass, squeezing it a bit, and spreading her cheeks apart. With my tongue already deep inside of her pussy I was kind of curious as to what he was doing. After seeing that nigga naked I kind of wanted a taste of him too, at that point. I had never noticed how sexy that nigga was before now. In one mind I wanted to push Kayla out of the way and just fuck him right in front of her face. However, yall know a nigga wasn't crazy enough to just go out and blow cover like that. I watched curiously as I continued to dig Kayla's pussy out with my tongue. He inched his self as close as he could get, almost literally putting his dick right in my face. I couldn't tell if he was doing it purposely or if he was just caught up trying to get at that fine specimen of ass in front of him, also known as Kayla. He then mustered up a good bit of spit and just let it run from his mouth down the crack of her ass. A good portion of it managed to find its way to my mouth and though somewhat disgusted I was kind of turned on at the same time. He then proceeded to finger and lick her asshole. With my now free hands I used one to play with Kayla's breast and the other to fondle the two rocks sitting up on my chest. Every once in a while, I couldn't help but to glance over at Big's dick. I figured that Kayla was well off in pleasure land so I decided to take a little adventure of my own. I abandoned my nipples and slowly made the advance for his dick. Just then Kayla's hand flew back giving Bigboy a brutal smack on the ass. Making his dick jump, I figured that it must somehow be a turn on for him. I took a brief break from my meal and moistened my lips, taking a deep breath before going back in, and then I went for it again. This time I was successful, getting a good handful of rock hard dick. Obviously thinking it was her stroking his dick he began talking shit to her.

"You like these tongues in that pussy and ass huh? You like how we eating you out ma? Take that dick out yo mouth and answer me bitch! You like this shit don't you," he said getting more aggressive with each question.

"Yeah muthafucka eat me, eat that shit good," Kayla snorted back not to be dominated by an almost complete stranger.

"Yeah I know you like this shit, keep sucking my niggas dick. Deep throat that big muthafucka," he responded slipping into a state of sexual euphoria. He leaned back over and again commenced flicking his tongue in, out, and around Kayla's asshole. While I continued doing the same thing to her pussy, and at the same time stroking his ever-hardening dick. This nigga had to be working with at least 10 inches or better.

After bout a good fifteen minutes of this shit niggas really started to flow with each other. At one point our tongues met and we both just sort of stopped for a sec and looked at each other like, "what the fuck," but just keep going. It was also at the point that he realized that I was stroking his dick and not

Kayla, but to my surprise he didn't seem to care. I even think I saw a slight grin spread across his face as he reached forward and pushed Kayla's head down on my shit.

"Suck my nigga's bitch," he said harshly while forcing two fingers into her ass, "That shit feeling kind of good my nigga. You want to do that favor for yo nigga son," he continued, lowering his tone and turning his attention to me.

Before I could answer his rock solid dick was smacking me in the face and begging for some attention. After playing with his dick I couldn't lie and say I don't roll like that. So I did what came natural and handled that shit for my nigga. He moaned appreciatively, momentarily licking Kayla's pussy, and then suddenly, he pulled away from me, slathered on some lube, and slid his long, thick, joint into Kayla's ass. I continued sucking his balls and licking her pussy at the same time. I knew Kayla, probably knew what was up by now, but fuck it we were all freaks in that bitch. She was taking my nigga's shit proudly for the first couple of minutes. Then he decided to kick shit into overdrive banging the fuck out of her till she could no longer contain herself. I slid from underneath them, playfully slapping my dick on both their asses before maneuvering myself in front of her face. Ordering her to suck my dick and give that ass up.

After ten minutes I decided that I'd had enough mouth action and was ready to bang some shit myself. She happily received my dick in her pussy as my homeboy laid down beside her and offered his dick to her mouth while he sucked her breast. I wasted no time in getting down to business banging the hell out of her pussy. My thick shaft gleefully stretched her tight pussy walls to the max as I rammed my manhood balls deep inside them. With my nigga's dick lodged deep in her throat Kayla latched onto my left ass cheek, squeezing as hard as she could, trying to control my hard, deep thrusts into her g-spot. My dick glistened with her sweet pussy juices, ultimately working as a natural lube. I watched blissfully as my nigga slid his joint in and out of her mouth.

"Fuck that pussy nigga," he said before grabbing hold of Kayla's head and ramming his rod down her throat. The site and basic experience of all this turned me on beyond words and I began a brutal assault on her pussy. The caramel skin of her plump pussy lips began to redden from the lustful

chastening I was giving her.

"Yeah fuck me nigga, fuck me," she managed to scream between gulps of Big's snake.

"You like my nigga's dick bitch?" Big asked aggressively.

"Fuck yeah!" she replied lustfully.

"Shut up and suck that dick hoe," I ordered before going on another rampage on her pussy. She let out a long exasperated groan as she gobbled down my nigga's pipe and happily received the beating I was putting on her pussy. "Yeah give me that fucking pussy. Take this big ass dick in that shit bitch." I continued.

About ten minutes later I slowed my pace and maneuvered myself into somewhat of a squatting position. I leaned down and began sucking on her free breast still not taking my eyes off the oral action she was giving my boy. Just then Big reached back and smacked my ass, ordering me to "Bang that shit." It caught me off guard but turned me on at the same time. As I leaned in to reclaim the nipple I'd reluctantly let go from the sudden impact of Big's hand against my ass. I could feel him slowly fondling my ass. I looked at him strangely but never broke the flow as I again began to plant a few solid licks to Kayla's g-spot.

"Mumm baby this shit feels so fucking good," she moaned.

"You ain't felt nothing yet bitch," Big interjected. Standing to his feet and stroking his dick he briefly stepped out of the room and a few minutes later he returned with his rock hard dick still in hand. "You ready for this surprise we got for you," he said with an almost alluring tone. He stepped up onto the bed behind me and grabbed my ass. "Damn son, when you gon let a nigga slide in this," he whispered. I looked back at him and smiled before pushing Kayla's legs back onto her chest and got a few more good strokes in before we switched positions again.

Once Kayla had slid all the way down on my dick Big began sliding his back into her ass. She yelped pleasurably from the sensation of the double penetration. I continued slowly deep-stroking her pussy from underneath while big tagged that ass.

"I been wanting this shit, for real son," he hissed while he ran his finger up the crack

of my ass. He moved in a lil closer. Digging deeper into Kayla's ass and letting his balls rub against mine. He grabbed another handful of my ass and proceeded to play with my asshole. Before I knew he'd slid the tip of his finger into my ass. Somehow I was able to let out a soft moan in spite of yelling out in pain. I started pushing up harder into ole girl's pussy lifting up a little as I started to change up my stroke. "I'm about to nut in this bitch's ass," he announced boastfully, "Aww fuck son, this shit tight as hell," he continued. With his finger completely in my ass I began pounding the hell out of that pussy and after a minute or so it started to feel good and I was coming near my own nut. I moaned loudly, alerting the world of my pending climax. "I want to see you bust that shit nigga," Big whispered before pulling his finger out of my ass. "Let's do this shit freak-style then my nigga," I said aloud. "Fasho my nigga." As he pulled out he rubbed the head of his dick up against my asshole, slightly applying pressure until it slid in. I jerked violently, grabbing Kayla's hips, and ramming my dick deep into her. He attempted to push in further and proceed to fuck me, but I was nowhere near ready for that. After taking about three or four more strokes he pulled out. I grunted loudly from the feeling and then withdrew my own manhood and joined Big in getting a last bit of head. Kayla seemed to take pride in servicing the both of us and it wasn't long before we had both busted in her mouth.

That night, after Big and I had taken Kayla on for about two more rounds of hardcore freaking, I decided to take her for one more. Her being the big ass freak she was she didn't give a fuck. So I fiercely feed this dick into her mouth making her gag hard as I fucked her face.

"Let's take this shit to the shower," I said stroking my dick as I withdrew it from her mouth.

"Ok, but I need this pussy beat a lil bit first," she replied wrapping her legs around my waist and pulling my dick into her tight, warm, moist pussy and I went into overdrive ramming my dick deep inside her walls.

"Damn this shit good," I groaned after a good ten minutes of pounding her creamy, wet cock box. I leaned over and grabbed her up off the couch keeping my dick inside her as I walked back to the bathroom.

"Damn nigga we got to do this more often," Kayla moaned as she worked her

pussy on my dick as I carried her into the shower. The warm water ran down in between us adding extra lube to her already wet pussy. "Shit I'm about to cum baby," she screamed.

"Bust that shit on this dick then baby."

"Oww...o...o...shit nigga."

"Give me that fucking pussy girl," I taunted aggressively between her moans and shouts. I put her down into doggy style so I could watch her cum ooze out and coat my dick while I beat the shit out of that pussy.

"Fuck me nigga! Fuck me, fuck me, fuck me muthafucka!" she chanted.

"This shit good to you baby?"

"Yeah nigga, fuck this pussy! Give me that big ass fucking dick!"

"You like this muthafuckin dick huh," I growled aggressively.

"Make this pussy cream nigga."

"Yeah cum on my dick baby, cum on this dick...oh shit."

"Yeah nigga make me cum."

"Fuck I'm about to bust baby girl," I announced in exasperated pleasure.

"Put that muthafucka in my ass before you cum nigga," she ordered. So I quickly pulled out and positioned myself over her with the head of my dick centered on her asshole. I slowly slid in while using my free hand to play with her pussy.

"I want you to cum in me nigga. I want all yo sweet nut in my fuckin ass," Kayla demanded as she began to rock back on my dick. Easing it further and further into her ass until it was finally balls deep inside her, "Fuck me nigga!"

"Give it up then!" I snapped back.

"Take it nigga, harder, harder, harder baby!"

"Fuck I'm about to nut!" I announced.

"Hold that shit nigga, this dick feeling good as hell."

I did my best to restrain it but I knew the eruption was coming soon. So I changed up my stroke a couple times pulling out to the tip and ramming it back in. Taking it a lil slower but hitting it harder each time.

"Shit nigga work this ass so I can feel that nut in me," she cried.

That was I needed to hear to send me into overdrive pounding that ass till my guts began to bubble and cum came rushing out like a flood. I slowly pulled out and watched as it dripped out of Kayla's ass and down her pussy. I then slid underneath her and licked her pussy clean getting a good taste of my own cum. She turned around getting into a 69 position so she could suck the last bit of cum out of my dick. She began slowly riding my tongue till she came to another climax and then sucked me off till I busted in her mouth. I could hear the phone ringing somewhere, but I was too far gone to even worry about looking for it.

"Now that's some good shit," she boasted continuing to slurp on my dick. "Damn this dick taste good," she said reaching for a towel to clean up with.

"Yeah you right about that shit."

After sucking my dick one last time Kayla went home and I finished up my shower. Once I had the temperature set just right I finally stepped in and let the hot water flow over me massaging my body and rinsing *away the remnants of the past couple hours. As I ran my hands up and down my body in aid to the hot water I began to replay the day's events in my head. A nigga had really put in that work today. That bitch Kayla had given my ass a fucking workout and a half, but I ain't complaining though, nigga was feeling that shit on the real. Especially when my nigga Big had come up in that bitch. Shit I got me some pussy and a lil dick on the slick side. But wait...hold up...does my nigga Big get down too? Hell up to this point I thought that the nigga was straight. Yet this nigga practically got down with me while we were messing around with ole girl. I mean first he let me suck his dick and then for a minute he actually had his shit up in me. Shit a nigga ain't gon lie man that shit stung like hell when he first got in but it started feeling good after a minute, but yo, what's really good? Does my nigga actually fuck around or was he just caught up in the moment? Man I don't know, but a nigga wouldn't mind finding out though. Just then I heard my iPad go off, breaking my train of thought. So I wrapped a towel around my waist and stepped out to get it. After retrieving it I saw a text from Big stating that he'd been trying to call me and asking where the hell I was. He apparently knew I in the house because my car was outside and Kayla had left the door open a lil bit. I texted him back and told him that I was in the shower and would be out in a few.*

No sooner than I had put the iPad on the counter I heard the TV in my room come to life. I finished rinsing the soap off my body, stepped out of the shower, and dried myself off. Then I went into the medicine cabinet and got out the cocoa butter and began messaging it into my skin. Hell yall know a nigga can't be walking around this muthafucka ashy and shit. I looked down at my dick and laughed to myself. "Boy you really had some fun today huh cuz," I laughed and continued to put more lotion on my tights and under my balls and on my ass. Over the years I've learned that cocoa butter does more than just give moisture it kind of gives your skin a little sweet taste. I wrapped the towel around my waist and proceeded to stand up and look in the mirror. "Damn son you need to lay off them chicken sandwiches a bit," I laughed noticing my once rock solid six pack was slipping to a semi-hard five and a half. Then just as I aimed for the doorknob I got another text from Big telling me to stop playing with myself and get in the room.

"I ain't got no need for that my nigga,"

I said as I walked into the room playfully punching him on the arm as I sat down on the bed next to him.

"Yeah you right about that son," he responded grabbing me by the waist and wrestling onto my back.

"Yo son what you doing," I said struggling to get loose."

"I want to finish what I started, you know me I never leave a job undone." Big replied, pining me down.

"What you mean dawg?"

"Man you know what I want," he said sliding his hand under my towel.

"Come on dawg, stop playing."

"Does this look like I'm playing," he continued pushing his finger into my ass and then aggressively biting my neck.

In one mind I wanted to resist but in the other I wanted more. When he saw I was no longer trying to fight him off he let up a little and proceeded to get to work on my nipples. I instinctively reach down and grabbed at his ass, but he jerked away saying I was grabbing for the wrong thing and then slid my hand down to his dick and instructed me to stroke.

"I'm about to really get up in this shit son, but don't worry I ain't gon hurt you babyboy. I'm a take my time with this because I been wanted to get this on the real son."

Ok...pause...now don't get me wrong I do mess around, been doing it for a couple years now, but a nigga really wasn't expecting this. Big is my muthafuckin nigga you dig, my homeboy from way, way back in the gap. Again, up to this point I was under the impression that the nigga straight. I guess you can never really know everything about a person huh?

"What's up dawg," Big said as he retreated from my nipples, noticing that I was a lil shook.

"Shit to be honest I'm a lil confused man. I mean I..."

"I got you," he said cutting me off, "I really ain't never did no shit like this but I been sort of curious about it ever since...ummm..."

"Ever since what son? Why are you stalling?"

"Since I found out that you do this shit," he blurted out quickly.

"What you mean? How you found that out?" I questioned, curious as to how he'd come to that conclusion but unable to deny it.

"I overheard this nigga talking one day bout this party and I just thought I would drop by for a minute."

"So what that got to do with me getting down?" I inquired.

"I'm getting to that son, hold on. So I got there and it was all niggas everywhere. Not a bitch in sight, and that's when I saw you with these two hardcore ass looking niggas getting off in the corner. At that point I ain't know what to do, so I just left, but the picture stayed with me, and earlier today when we were fucking that bitch and you grabbed my dick I had a flashback to that night and wanted to test you out," he explained.

"Damn so you found a nigga out huh," I laughed nervously.

"Yeah I guess so son," Big laughed.

"So what's up then?" I conceded.

"Shit I think you already know the answer to that my nigga." I looked down to see him at full mass, somewhere in the mix he'd managed to slip out of his clothes.

"Damn son I ain't know you was... damn, damn shit that's all I can say," I stated.

"Yo let's just rock this shit my nigga, we'll talk later."

"Fasho son," I said as I got down between his legs and began sucking his dick.

"Ahh fuck nigga, that shit feel good as hell," Big moaned.

"Shit taste good too son," I replied before taking another dive down on my niggas massive pole.

"Damn homie you better than ole girl we was fuckin earlier. Shit nigga, suck on them balls for me son."

"You like that shit my nigga," I said as I took his balls into my mouth while stroking his dick. He threw his head back and closed his eyes moaning in appreciation. I then lifted his balls and flicked my tongue over his asshole.

"Oh shit nigga what you doing...damn yo...oh shit! Keep stroking my dick while you doing that shit son."

Bout fifteen minutes later my nigga was deep up in my shit banging the hell out of my ass. Shit kind of hurt a lil at first but started feeling good as hell after a while.

"You like this shit nigga," he asked.

"Fuck yeah son," I answered aggressively.

"Oh fuck nigga, this some good shit for real cuz. Almost make a nigga want to nut quick yo," Big stated.

"Go head and get that shit then my nigga. Bust that shit right here on my chest yo," I barked lustfully.

"Damn kid you ready for it?"

"Hell yeah nigga, go head and get you."

"Aww shit...damn nigga I'm getting close!" he exclaimed, pounding harder with every stroke.

"Fuck yeah nigga, fuck this ass like it's yours nigga," I moaned, clinching onto him.

"Fuck yeah nigga! You want it! You ready for this nut son."

"Hell yeah nigga! Beat this shit up muthafucka! Give me that dick son," I yelled aggressively.

"Fuck I'm about to cum dawg!"

"Get that shit then nigga."

"Aww shit...I'm cumin yo!"

"Bust that shit in my ass nigga...shit that dick felt good nigga."

No less than five minutes later I felt Big's dick start to twitch as his hot cum filled my hole. I dug my nails into his back and begged for more as he attempted to pull out. I was still a little shocked from what happened earlier and now this. I wasn't sure how to compute it all in my head, but I will admit that I loved every minute of it and wouldn't hesitate to do it all again.

"You liked this dick son?" Big asked.

"Hell fucking yeah son, you can hit this shit whenever you want my nigga."

"Aight, I'm a hold you to that shit son," he laughed, looking directly into my eyes.

"Fasho... now let's do that shit again," I exclaimed, wiggling my ass around on his dick which was still deep inside me.

Ty Eros

Special Delivery

SPECIAL DELIVERY

It's Friday morning and the supplies I ordered still haven't arrived. According to the UPS website the boxes have been on the truck for delivery since four forty-five this morning. However, it's almost ten thirty and not one of the UPS trucks I've seen so far has stopped and delivered anything here. Yes, I know there's a six-hour window for them to get here, but hell I think I might have done better going to the local office and picking it up myself. Other than this I've pretty much got everything done and ready for tonight so maybe that's why I'm so anxious. Not to mention this is the first time that Ty has put something almost totally in my hands and I damn sure didn't want to drop the ball. As much as I loved the occasional dick in my ass I doubt I would enjoy a foot or whatever else Ty might try and shove up there if I fucked up his night.

"Come get it, come get it, come get it if you ready! Come get it, come get it, come and get this good shit! Come get...," my phone

116

*sang, echoing through the loft till I picked it
up.*

"What's good my dude," I answered
hurriedly.

"I just got on the bus headed to
Alpharetta, what was the salesperson's name
that I needed to talk to?" Sam asked.

"Ask for Rico or Sheena, they will
know what you need. Rico will actually be one
of the guys dancing at the party tonight so I'm
sure he'll take care of you," I replied.

"Oh really, is that the sexy, slim, kind
of toned nigga Ty was smashing in the office
last night," he exclaimed.

"Nah that's his partner, Rico is the
dark skinned brother," I stated.

"Ok... shit he was sexy too! You think
he'll let me smash tonight," he inquired with
a grin I could hear through the phone.

"Well I know that both of them are
versatile but that's something you'll have to
discuss with him," I laughed.

"Aight, aight well let me get off this phone so I don't miss this place and end up walking or asking some embarrassing questions," Sam joked.

"Ok, I'm still here waiting for UPS to show with the toys and shit. Hit me back if you have any trouble, maybe I can swing out there after a while," I said, peeking out the office window.

"Damn, the email did say between 6:15 and noon right?" he asked.

"Yea," I answered dryly.

"Well knowing how they run back home it'll probably be closer to noon when they get there. Don't stress though bruh, they're coming and I'll help you finish setting things up when I get back," Sam stated, trying to calm my nerves.

"You got to get yourself ready bruh," I exclaimed.

"Don't worry about that, I got this and you're gonna be fine," he said sternly, letting

me know that he wasn't backing down.

"If you say so bruh, let me get off here and do some shit. I think I'll check on the other dancer I interviewed yesterday. He seemed a little disappointed that he didn't get the gig," I said.

"Look at you trying to be the nice guy," Sam joked.

"Not really I thought he was good and had a nice body but he was just too nervous and his dick wouldn't get hard. Plus, I need to do something to take my mind off of this shipment and you need to pay attention to where you're going," I replied.

"True, well I'll talk to you later bruh," he said.

"Yea, stay dry out there nigga," I stated, before hanging up.

Moments later I received a text from Sam asking what I meant. I texted him back and said, "The thirst is real and vultures are always out lol." Obviously he didn't like my joke because he didn't reply, but after I said it I thought it was kind of lame too. Then just as I was getting ready to take a seat at the desk the door buzzed.

"Hello, this is UPS I have a package for Mr. Devon Willis," a male voice echoed through the loft.

"Finally," I said to myself, "Come on up man," I said, opening the gate for him.

I felt a huge weight drop off my shoulders as I listened to him making his way up the stairs. Only thing I had to do now was sort through it all and make sure it was all there so I could put the bags and displays together. Then right as I heard the thump of the hand truck on the last step there was a loud crash. So I rushed out the door to see a busted box lying next to the hottest piece of chocolate I think I've ever seen.

"Man I really apologize about your package I thought I was clear that top step but my foot got caught and..."

"Hey it's ok, don't worry about it, the

main question is are you ok?" I interrupted, reaching out a hand to help him to his feet.

"Yea I'm good thanks, my ass and that box kind broke my fall," he joked nervously.

"Well, let's get this mess up and once everybody is inside we can take a second look just to make sure," I said, quickly grabbing everything I could off of the floor.

"Ok that sounds like a plan and I apologize again man, I hope nothing was damaged," he stated, placing the box back on the stack and wheeling the hand truck to the door.

"Seems like the box took the brunt of the damage," I replied, shuffling around to pick up any stray pieces from his path.

"So ummm... I know this may be awkward but what's up with all the sex toys? You know what I'm sorry I shouldn't have asked you that," he said, anxiously fidgeting with his handheld.

"It's ok man, we run an adult

entertainment company and tonight we're having a little event here at the loft. Some of the toys will be prizes and the others will be bagged as party favors," I replied.

"Damn that's a big ass dildo," he commented, looking at the toys in my arms, "But you said adult entertainment, do you mean like porn or something else," he added.

"The owner Ty Eros did some amateur porn a few years back, but now he writes erotica and we host parties and different kinds of adult oriented fun," I answered, doing my best to explain it without giving too much and weirding him out.

"Ok, I see so was this gay or straight porn?" he inquired.

"It was gay porn, and we cater to black men, most are very discreet, professionals, people who you wouldn't think of as gay or bi," I said candidly.

"Ok so would you think I was bi?" he asked suddenly after tapping around on his handheld for a minute.

"Well no initially but the comment you made about your ass was a bit suspect and the way you're eyeing those toys says a little bit too," I responded.

"Ha, ha that's funny, but I'll admit I am a bit curious," he laughed, "I'm Davion by the way," he added.

"Nice to meet you Davion, and you don't seem to be from around here, but what are you curious about," I asked taking in the sight of his solidly build muscular frame.

"Is that thing gonna go in somebody's ass? I mean my shit is pretty big but just seeing that kind of makes me nervous," he laughed.

"It will if anybody is bold enough to try it, my homebody has a pretty thick dick but yeah man that's the type of shit that'll ruin some walls," I laughed.

"So you and your boy used to mess around? I mean forgive me if I'm asking too many questions, but shit you look like you got some good... man I'm sorry I should go,"

Davion said, reaching me the handheld and stylus to sign for the package.

"No worries man, you're fine, and yes we did and I've never had any complaints from anybody. You seem like you have a pretty nice body under that uniform, you never wanted to try porn or dancing?" I asked, signing and handing back the stylus, "Wait a minute did you just say you have a big dick," I added.

"I thought about it but I was always nervous about somebody noticing me on the street and putting my business out. My body is ok and yea I kind of slid that in," he laughed, "but I don't want to hold you up man, I've probably been here longer than I need to be anyway," he continued.

"So you just gon bring yo sexy ass in here, flirt with a nigga, and leave," I stated, with a grin.

"I mean I'd like to do more but I don't want to take too…"

"Don't worry about that," I

interjected, "I figured I was going to be waiting another hour or so anyway and besides that I want to make sure you didn't hurt yourself when you fell," I added, stepping around and closing the door behind him.

"Oh I'm good I'll just take it easy the rest of the day and put an ice pack on it when I get back to the hotel," Davion said.

"Hotel? So you really aren't from here?" I reiterated.

"Nah I go back home Sunday morning I'm just out here doing some training, but my trainee called out today so I'm flying solo," he answered.

"Oh I see, so where are you from, if you don't mind me asking," I continued to probe, stepping closer to him.

"I'm from Louisiana, but look I don't want to come off too bold, but... man that ass is looking real good bruh," Davion replied, licking his lips as he spoke.

"Oh really... well how bout I give you a better view," I said, turning my back to him and bending over slightly.

"Damn you gon tease me now huh," he laughed.

"Nah I just wanted you to get a better view since you seem to like it," I stated, standing upright again before moving over to the futon and getting on my knees.

"I definitely like it... I'm just trying not to start nothing we can't finish," he replied, fighting a losing battle to resist the urge to keep watching.

"Just pass me that oil off the table," I instructed while sliding down the sweats I was wearing.

"Damn bruh, I probably shouldn't but I can't help it yo," Davion said, oiling up his hands and firmly gripping my cheeks.

"See I knew you... oh shit nigga," I moaned as my thoughts were interrupted by Davion's tongue wiggling into my hole.

A few minutes later I found out for myself how big Davion's dick really was. It was mad thick like Sam's and had to be at least six or seven inches long and it wasn't even hard. I timidly stroked it to life while he proceeded to fondle my ass. His plump finger slowly invaded my moistening hole and all I could do was moan softly as I firmly gripped his hardening dick. My mouth began to water at the thought of tasting the super king-sized piece of chocolate I had in my hand. Then just as I was about to give it a big wet kiss he pulled away.

"You know I'd love to see one of these slid in that ass," Davion said, sifting through the conveniently open box of toys.

"Why use a toy when you got a real dick hanging between your legs," I stated brazenly.

"I don't know if you ready for that bruh, that hole feels a little tight," he laughed.

"My shit is always tight son," I snapped back, "and clean too," I added.

"Well hell if it wasn't I would already have shit crumbs in my mouth," he joked.

"You ain't funny nigga, and don't you have a route to get back to," I said coldly.

"Oh now you want me to leave," Davion laughed.

"Nah I want your sexy ass to fuck me but you want to play with the dildos," I retorted.

"Well good things come to those who wait right? At least that's what I think they used to say," he stated with a big grin on his face.

"Ok I get it... you're attractive, got a nice body, a big dick, and you try to be slick too," I replied.

"Nah I'm aight and the only thing slick about me is this dick once I get it deep inside these pretty cakes you got," he said, still smiling like he had just gotten lucky.

"Humm... I bet it will be," I answered, biting on my bottom lip as I watched him walk *back towards me.*

"Well I'm trying to find out but you acting like you don't want to have no fun with a nigga," he countered, sitting the dildo down on the table and grabbing the oil again.

"I do want to have fun, but if I'm going to have something in my ass I just prefer a real dick," I said, "But umm sir... what you think you about to do with that," I questioned.

"I could put it back if it's a problem, I just wanted to see that hole get opened up a lil bit and have some fun before we really get to business," Davion replied, putting the oil back down and picking the dildo back up.

"I don't have a problem with it but that stuff was brought for the party and I haven't had a chance to do an inventory to make sure it's all there. Not to mention it's Ty's money that paid for it and he'll probably flip if he walked in here and caught me test driving the toys," I explained, trying not to sound like a stick in the mud.

"Ok I got you, I'll go put it..."

"Nah, nah it's ok... go head and open it, I'm sure we have enough shit in those boxes to go around tonight," I said, interrupting him.

"Are you sure? I mean a second ago you were against it so why the sudden change of heart?" he inquired.

"Let's just say I'm a lil curious and part of me just really wants to give you what you want. Plus, it's only one dildo," I stated, sliding my pants all the way off and arching my back.

"Well I don't you to get in any trouble with Ty or whoever..."

"Stop talking and take your clothes off nigga," I snapped, cutting him off.

Not more than a minute later Davion was completely naked and kneeling beside me squeezing and smacking my ass with one hand while he lubed me up with the other. I picked up where I left off and slowly began kissing and licking the head of his dick as I stroked it. Again he gently began to finger me this time *stretching me a little further using two fingers. The feeling of my hole being fondled and the scent of Davion's manhood sent chills up and down my spine. Having been fucked a couple times in the last two days by Sam it was a bit easier for me to open up. However, those long, plump digits wiggling around inside me still stung a little at first. To take my mind off the initial pain I just arched my back a little more and stuffed my mouth with dick to muffle my moans. There was a slight saltiness to it but yet it was still sweet and seemed to melt in my mouth in like an everlasting lollipop. As he got harder it appeared to keep growing, almost gagging me as I attempted to take it down my throat. Then once again I was robbed of the pleasure of being fingered, but I wasn't going to allow him to steal that chocolate from my jaws. I could tell he was struggling a bit trying to reach over me but I didn't care. I just kept my eyes closed and continued to give him my version of the best blowjob he'd ever had. Skillfully milking every inch of it with my lips while I massaged it with my tongue and gently cupped his balls in my hand. With every stroke I could feel his dick pulsing and inviting itself deeper. Each time treating me with a shot of honey-like precum. Capturing me in the spell of its addictive essence that was meant to be savored fully and completely. Hearing the cracking of plastic and no longer feeling the strain of him pulling away I figured he'd achieved his mission. Then came the dull humming buzzing of the toy. I was surprised it came with batteries but that was good news to me. At the instant when the tip of it made contact with my body I didn't know what to feel as he slowly guided it between my cheeks. I began sucking more aggressively and he toyed with me even more. Smacking my ass and dipping the tip of the dildo inside me. Sometimes going a little deeper and others just barely touching my skin, but the sensation was driving me crazy. Finally, he pushed it about halfway in, from what I could tell, causing me to pull back off his dick and grunt loudly. The dildo was only about as thick as two manly fingers put together but it was nearly nine inches of vibrating metal.*

"Damn you got a nice grip in that shit

son, when the last time you had some dick,"
Davion asked as he worked the dildo deeper
inside me.

"Shit... last night, my homeboy Sam
fucked the sense out of this ass," I replied,
rambling in a euphoric trance.

"Really and yo shit still tight like this?
You really got that snapback huh," he stated
in disbelief.

"Fuck yea, this grade A ass nigga,
always tight, always clean, always ready," I
said before releasing another loud grunt.

"Damn homie, this looks good as fuck
though," Davion moaned lustfully, "and that
mouth is on point too son, I need a homie like
you back home," he continued, kissing my
cheeks while he proceeded to work the entire
length of the dildo in and out of me.

"You just talking shit cause you ready
to fuck nigga, but I'll let you get away with it
for now," I stated, winding my hips back as
my inner dick started to take over.

"Humm you're funny dude, but I do want to fuck now for real, for real," he admitted, standing upright again and giggling his dick around in my thirsty mouth.

"What's funny, you fuck me today, go home Sunday, slip up in yo regulars, and you gon forget all about this ass. So why embellish the obvious when I'm already gonna give you the ass nigga," I countered, feeling my ass getting wetter by the second.

"Aight I see you don't like niggas to be real with you bruh. You say I'm talking shit but I'm just calling it like I see it, hell I already know this ass is good and I ain't even got in it yet," he stated.

"Well... stop talking and... and... fuck me yo..." I stammered.

A few minutes later Davion was giving me just what I asked for, filling my guts with that thick, long dick. I'd only met a handful of guys that had a big dick and a nice stroke game. From the moment he slid the head in I knew I was in for a good workout. I was certain that he was getting treat too as my tight, warm walls gripped his pipe. Sucking it in deeper with every thrust, forcing him to fuck me harder and harder as I began to cream on his dick. Lost in ecstasy I sang out a vociferous tune of pleasure. If there had been any neighbors on the other side of those walls they would have no doubt hear me yelling, screaming, moaning, and demanding Davion to pound me deep and pound me hard. The clock on the wall ticked spitefully loud letting us know that our time was getting short but I didn't want him to stop. At that moment if Ty, Sam, or anybody else would have come in I wouldn't have even cared. Shit they could have joined in if they wanted to as long as they knew I wasn't sharing this good dick I was getting. Wanting to feel him deeper I flipped over on my back and allowed him to pin my legs back to my shoulders. Being flexible as hell it only made my ass more assessable and my hole open up even more him. I could feel myself creaming again as I grasped his muscular arms. Digging my fingers into his skin and slipping off into licentious bliss while the minutes faded into memories.

Another twenty minutes or so passed and I was in control now. Bouncing up and down and grinding my hips like stripper on a pole. In the mirror on the wall behind us I could see just how wet my ass was. Davion's thick, black log was dripping with my creamy nectar, acting as a natural lubricant while clasped onto his pecs and slammed this ass down in his lap. Taking that dick down to the balls and then sliding all the way to the head before dropping back down to the balls again. Davion grasped my cakes tightly in an effort to try and gain back a little control, adamantly exclaiming that I was going to make him nut if I kept riding his dick like that. However, making him cum was exactly what I wanted. I knew our time was running short plus I still had a lot of shit to get done before Ty came in the office. Not to mention that at any moment Sam might have called because he needed me to come get him or something. Still the feeling of my hole being impaled was slightly overriding my sense of sagaciousness. Every bit of my logic and reason was flying out the window while I indulged myself on a stranger's dick. It was some good dick though, if I may add, just in case I didn't make that clear already.

"Ah fuck son I'm about to cum for real," Davion cried, using every ounce of strength he had to pry me off of him.

"Give me that shit then nigga," I snapped, dropping to my knees with my mouth wide open and my tongue hanging out.

"Oh shit! Oh shit! Oh shit!" he repeated over and over again, each time with more intensity as hot streams of man-milk shot into my mouth and spattered onto my face.

Noticing that he was still hard I seized the opportunity to get every last drop of cum I could get out of that dick before laying on my back and begging him to fuck me till I came. Obviously not one to disappoint Davion slipped his rock back inside me and pumped me slow and deep while I proceeded to stroke my own dick. His thick rod caressing my hole sent me right back into ecstasy. I reached around with my free hand and grasped onto his hip, forcing him deeper. Wanting more I spread my legs back even wider and began working my hips to meet his strokes.

"Come get it, come get it, come get it if you ready! Come get it, come get it, come get this good shit," I heard my phone singing in the background. Even though I knew it was probably Sam I couldn't stop to answer it at that moment. I didn't want to stop till I busted my nut.

Moments later the room was quiet again with the exception of my grunts and moans. Outside of the events Ty hosted and other sex parties I went to I'd never met a guy one minute and then had his dick in me the next. However, I think that's what made the sex with Davion even better. The suspense of time running out as well as this sexy chocolate muthafucka walking in our door and boldly hitting on me. I had my thoughts about him too when I first saw him but I doubt I would have acted on them beyond a little flirting if he hadn't opened that door. The box of sex toys busting open was an awkward but convenient icebreaker too. Besides that, it was just something about being in Atlanta that made men throw caution to the wind, myself included.

As I neared my climax part of me was starting to feel a little guilty for ignoring that phone call. Yet the sensation of Davion's dick massing my prostate quickly dispelled it. I started to moan even louder anticipating the pending eruption. Davion obliged my unspoken request by taking subtlety longer and harder strokes. I grabbed a handful of his ass and squeezed it like my life depended on it. Closer and closer I could feel it coming, my nut was quickly rising up and I couldn't fight it. Wanting to enjoy getting fucked a bit longer I paced my strokes and held tighter to Davion. Eventually I just let my dick go and allowed Davion to pound me real good until the cum came flooding out of my dick onto my stomach. I kept a grip on his ass cheeks to let him know I wanted him to keep going. He obliged and a few moments later a few more jets of nut came shooting out of me. Followed almost instantaneously by Davion giving me another shower with his hot jizz. I was almost too worn out to move but I knew I had to clean this shit up and Davion had to get back to his route. So after a minute or two I hopped up and made my way to the bathroom with Davion on right behind. We both cleaned up, got dressed, and said our goodbyes. He apologized again for banging up the box, but once again I told him not to worry about it and invited him to the event tonight. It may have been a long shot but I went ahead and added him to the guest list anyway, just in case.

"Come get it, come get it, come get if you ready! Come get…" my phone began singing again, this time I knew for it was Sam.

"Nigga what you doing this my third time calling you son," Sam barked before I could get a word out.

"UPS finally came, the guy fell coming up the stairs and busted up one of the boxes and it was a mess man. Thankfully he was ok and from what I can tell so far the merchandise is ok too," I explained.

"Oh ok, you could have at least picked up and said you'll call me back or texted me," *he scolded.*

"Yea you're right, everything just happened so fast though. Anyway how did it go in Alpharetta?" I asked changing the subject.

"That's why I was calling you to let you know what happened but I'm almost halfway back to the loft now I guess. So I'll just tell you about it and show you the outfit Rico hooked up for me when I get there," he replied.

"Ok cool, I need to get out of here and run some errands since the delivery has been made, maybe I can just scoop you up from one of the stations and we can go grab something to eat," I stated, looking at the clock and realizing I still needed to go pick up the liquor and few other last minute things.

"Aight just hit me up or I'll call you to see where you are so we can connect," Sam stated.

About fifteen minutes later I had reorganized the front of the loft and was on my way out the door. It was now almost 1:30 and I knew traffic would be a mess soon so I needed to get going. Security and the caterers would both be arriving in about five hours and the loft needed to be ready. I was sure that Ty would be in the office by the time I got back so I grabbed the to-do list off the desk and stuffed it in my pocket. Feeling a little naked I grabbed a short-sleeve button up out of Ty's closet and just put it over my tank and sweats. Then I went back into the bathroom to brush my teeth and take a final look at myself. The ride from Alpharetta to the first train station was nearly thirty minutes and then Sam would have to hop on red line headed south. So I figured I had at least a half hour before I would hear from him. The liquor store was about a ten minute drive from the loft and then I needed to pick up some extra face towels and mini soap bars. If I played my cards right and timed everything good I should be ok. Then just as I was about to walk out the door my work phone rang.

"Wyldcard Entertainment, this is Devon," I answered professionally.

"Drop the formality kid it's me," Ty laughed, "I figured you'd be out and about so I didn't bother calling the office. Anyway I had a meeting with Mike and Que and we just may have another VIP to add to the list. Don't worry about it though I'll take care of it when I get to the office, I just wanted to keep you in the loop. Catering, security, and the dancers should all get there between six and seven right?" he continued, ending with a question.

"Yes, security should arrive first, maybe about 6:15 at the latest, then catering will be there to setup at 6:30, dancers are scheduled for seven, and guest will probably trickle in between 7:30 and 8pm, when the event actually starts," I replied, mentally going through the itinerary.

"Ok great, I'll be there in about maybe two hours, hopefully you get back before me or around the same time so we can make sure the loft is ready for everybody. How about Sam? Is he good?" Ty continued to inquire.

"Yes he's all together he went out to Alpharetta this morning and Rico fitted him

up. I'm actually gonna pick him up from the train station in about half an hour. I had planned to get us lunch since I know neither of us have eaten today but..."

"Yea 86 that idea I need you back at the loft ASAP. I'll stop and get us all something to eat on my way then after the event we can all go out to eat somewhere. So do what you have to do, pick him up, and get back to the loft as soon as you can. We'll probably use my room as the changing area for the dancers so I'll tend that. Aight well I know you have a lot to do and I have some other calls and stops to make as well so I'll talk to you later," Ty instructed before he hung up.

Man what a day and it really hasn't even gotten started yet. I could only hope everything worked out well tonight since the brunt of it was in my hands. Sam probably wasn't gonna be happy that we weren't eating yet but he'll get over it. Hell I had to do my job and Ty wasn't about to get in my ass for slacking or fucking up his event tonight. Anyway, let me get my ass out the door before

I get any other surprises. Even though I'm a little behind I'm still confident I can get it all done, plus whatever else Ty throws at me between now and tonight. Man hell with all that, this is gonna be a fun, stress-free night and I'm going to make sure of it.

Ty Eros

Stranger Knocking

Sitting at my desk I could hear footsteps
Thump, thud, coming closer and closer
No buzzer was heard, no calls made
Who was this trespasser in my building
Boom, boom, boom, boom, boom
The sound of a fist pounding against the door
Perplexed and leery I ask for an identity
A muffled masculine voice echoes in the hall
The unscripted nature of the visit made me uneasy but I
shook with anticipation
Curiosity was overtaking my nervousness
Slowly the door opened and there he was
Tall, sexy, muscular, a bright smile, and a twinkle of
mischief in his eyes
But why was this strange piece of eye candy here
Politely I said hello, but was quickly knocked to the floor
by hard blow to the face
I opened my eyes and found myself tied up, gagged, and all
alone
My clothes had been ripped off and there was a sharp
stinging feeling in my ass
Mouth was bloody and my head hurt
Just as quickly as he came he was gone and I had been
beaten and raped
Though I would have willingly let him fuck me
I was left on the floor with my boxers in mouth and an ass
full of cum
I wiggled lose but was too shocked to move
A knock on the door I'll never forget

CASTING
Calling all sexy black men with an appetite for the hot, wet, and freaky. Must be 18 or older to apply.
DIRECTOR
DAY

<u>CASTING DAY</u>

My homeboy Devon only had today and tomorrow left to get everything ready for the party and he still hadn't booked the dancers. I was on board with hosting and Ty had given Devon the go ahead to process everything so I could get paid. That, however, was after he caught Devon sucking my dick in the bathroom and then watched us fuck on the couch. I thought it was strange, but I wanted some ass anyway and he didn't seem like the type to take no for answer. Anyway, from the glance I got of the to-do list that was left for Devon, Ty wanted at least two dancers for some kind of live show right before the main event. I had never been to a party like this but it seemed like it was gonna be something to remember. They were booking strippers, had a lineup of games and prizes, catering, security, and the guest list was full of sexy, discreet professionals that didn't mind spending a dime on some hot shit. At least that's what Devon told me when I asked about the thirty-dollar cover. The VIP list was pretty interesting too, two casting directors from major porn companies, two porn stars, and three other dudes that spent the extra penny to get on it. Devon told me these guys would all need to be escorted to Ty's suite when they arrived and outside of who they were and where to put them that was all he knew. I figured Ty probably had something up his sleeve or just didn't trust Devon to handle the whole event.

So anyway like I said earlier, there was supposed to be dancers booked for some kind of live show before the real show got started. In my mind all I could see was some guys twerking and gyrating all over the guest and maybe a lil on stage play to entertain the crowd, but I guess I'll see what's really up tomorrow night. Still, as of now all we had was a few auditions scheduled and nobody booked yet. Anyway, let me go head and get to the point. Ok, so I was in the guestroom chillin when I heard music playing from the front of the loft. So like I said Ty and Devon would be auditioning guys for tomorrow night, so I figured that's what was going on so I decided to go take a peek. Hell I didn't have anything else to do, so why not go be nosey for a minute? So I grabbed a pair of shorts to put on and made my way down the hall. When I got close enough I could see this dark skin dude with a pretty nice body standing in front of Ty and Devon stroking his dick while he winded hips to the music. They both just sat there looking sort of stoically as the dude went through his routine. At first I was like damn they a hard audience, but then I saw what their attentions were fixed on. I had been standing there for at least five minutes now and dude had been stroking but his dick wasn't getting hard. I mean it happens sometimes but shit this wasn't one of those times when you'd want your shit to be limp. He could have been nervous too, but hell you knew what you were getting into when you answered that phone yesterday. Now maybe dude just needed some help but from the looks on Ty and Devon's faces they weren't impressed and that wasn't happening. So I went back to the room and laid down. I actually feel kind of bad for the dude but oh well I guess.

About an hour or so later I woke up feeling a little hungry so I thought I would go try and raid the fridge. I didn't hear anymore music so I figured the auditions must have been over. However, what I saw when I got up the hall was quite the opposite, or maybe just the end result of a good one. Masculine moans and shit talk echoed through the loft causing my dick to get brick and forget all about how hungry I was. I peered around the corner to see two sexy ass mofos getting it in on the floor in front of Ty. I immediately thought back to my first encounter with him after he'd caught me and Devon in the bathroom. He was a weird freaky type of dude but still kind of sexy in his own way. Anyway, I saw these two dudes down on the floor getting it like their lives depended on it. I looked around but I didn't see Devon anywhere, so I figured Ty must have sent him out for a minute while he indulged in a lil voyeurism. The guys didn't seem to mind though. They were both sexy and the homie was taking ole boy's dick with ease, and from what I could see it was a decent size. They both looked like they worked out regularly but the one on his back seemed to have the better body. He had to be maybe 5'6 or 5'7 maybe a little taller, kind of hard to tell when somebody is on the floor with their legs in the air. Anyway, he had smooth, milk chocolate looking skin, neatly braided, shoulder-length dreads, and nicely defined muscles. The other guy was about my height, I guess, had velvety, dark skin, a little thicker than the other one but you could tell by the size and tone of his arms that he hit the iron pretty often. His pecs sat up proudly from his solid frame, outlining his core and flexing impressively as his drove his thick dick deep into his partner's gut. From the look on Ty's face I could tell he was enjoying the sight, licking his full lips while his eyes were fixed in a lustful gaze. I couldn't blame him though, seeing those two kind of turned me on too. I actually wanted to get closer and get a better view of the action but I figured it might have been best for me to hang back. Ty might have tried to get me involved, not that I would have minded at this point but I didn't want to give Ty any incentive to test me any further he already had.

About ten minutes later the boys had changed positions and Ty was no longer sitting on the sideline. I kind of figured he was going to join in at some point. To be honest I wanted to run out there and stick my dick in somebody's mouth too. Shit for a moment I was feeling a lil jelly as I watched king chocolate pound his homie doggy style while they both spit shined Ty's dick. Something I had only had happen to me maybe once or twice. I guess being the boss really did have its perks in this case. At that moment I wondered if this dude had ever smashed Devon, not really my business I guess, but if he dicking down his other employees, or potential employees, who's to say he hasn't fucked my boy. Maybe I'll ask him one day. Anyway, yea I got a little sidetracked, but we're good now. So I stepped away for a minute because I really was kind of getting jealous. When I returned Ty was long stroking that ass while he lapped at big chocolate's hole. The sounds of sex echoed tauntingly as I watched in silence. Hearing the words "fuck me nigga," over and over had my dick aching and leaking with anticipation. Then the thought of what would happen if I was to get caught standing here peeking and rubbing my dick hit me. Maybe I'd be forced to join in, but then again you can't really force the willing right? My stomach grumbled reminding me of why I'd gotten up in the first place but the pulsing erection I had pushed hunger to the side. Plus, I could tell that was some good ass Ty was getting by the way he stroked, probably trying to hold that nut back so he could keep fucking longer. The way he was sucking that dick made me think twice about not running up in there and whipping my shit out too. I didn't know too many tops that could suck dick like that but damn, this nigga seemed to be good. Big chocolate just stood there pinching his nipples with his eyes closed, slowly grinding his hips to meet the rhythm of Ty's strokes. Those pretty cakes of his clinched tight every time Ty took him down to the balls. Then as if it was all a big freaky chain reaction dicks began to spit and splatter cum everywhere. First it was the bottom, shooting his shit on the floor, then big chocolate and Ty came almost simultaneously. Right when Ty pulled out and began to spray the bottom dude's ass with cum, sexy chocolate let his lose all over Ty's face, chest, and the back of his partner.

"Go head and right up the paperwork, these two will be perfect," Ty said as Devon came in the door.

"Well fuck what did I miss," he shrieked, walking over to the table and putting down his keys and the bags he had in hand.

"Some hot shit," I thought to myself, watching the frustrated expression on his face turn to a grin when he spotted me.

"I guess I'll see what other talents these guys have at the event," he stated, walking through handing out towels from one of the bags like it was normal. I guess seeing me peeping around the corner he knew he could get the details from me, but then again who knows how often this type of shit happened here.

"I can definitely say they both give some good ass head and this one here has some good tight ass," Ty commented,

slapping his still semi-erect dick against the dude's ass.

"I can only imagine, but ummm yall go head and clean up so we can get this paperwork done for yall. The bathroom is the first door to the left down that hall," Devon replied, pointing towards it as he spoke and I took that as my que to get my ass back to the room before anybody else saw me.

I didn't know how long Devon had been gone and all, but I did know that the twenty minutes or so I stood there watching was definitely a hot sight to see, especially the ending. Not to mention how Ty didn't seem to mind having cum all over him. That nigga was definitely a freak and I was sure in the right moment he might give up those cakes too. That could just be wishful thinking though, since I was slightly attracted to him now. Even though I sucked dick and got my ass ate on occasion I still wasn't about to let nobody fuck me. The only person that ever came close was Devon and that was in the heat of the moment because he had done ate the fuck out of my shit for bout fifteen minutes and then started grinding on it which was cool till I felt him slip in a bit. That shit stung like hell and almost turned me off, but yall know I got that ass back when I bent him over. In addition to that, seeing those niggas getting it in like that sort of gave me an idea of what I would see once the party got started. I still a little nervous about that but I guess once hormones start flowing and shit I'll be fine. Now I wondered what the last interview was gon do because Ty had already hired his two guys for the show. I knew I definitely wanted to get a taste of that brown skin nigga and the thick chocolate one could get it too.

"Aight I saw you peeking like a kind when I came in so go head tell it nigga," Devon announced as busted in the room.

"Man look, I was just going to get me a snack from the kitchen but instead I got an eyeful," I answered.

"Ok so tell me what you saw and don't leave anything out," he insisted.

"I'll tell you if you help me with this," I replied, laying across the bed clinching my

throbbing dick.

"Well the guys are gone, Ty is in the shower, and the next appointment isn't till four so I don't mind," Devon stated.

"Damn that was quick," I said.

"I already had the paperwork ready before the auditions started this morning, and you already know how quick a nigga can roll out after he gets his nut," he answered.

"Damn you still remember that huh," I laughed.

"Oh yea I remember my nigga, you left me with my pants down and an ass full of cum," Devon shot back.

"Ok, ok I guess I deserved that," but shit, if yall already have what you need for the party, why hold another audition," I asked.

"This last one is for insurance if he makes the cut, but enough of that tell me what when on while I was gone," he said, changing the subject back to me and what I had seen.

"You got to hold up your end of the bargain first," I said with a smile.

"Oh don't worry my nigga, I got you, go head and start talking while I get these shorts off you," he assured me as he kneeled next to me on the bed.

"Well I don't know if I can think, talk, and get head all the same time," I joked, grabbing a handful of ass while he took me into his mouth.

"I guess that means I need to stop then huh," he laughed.

"Nah man don't do that... fuck..." I moaned, savoring the feeling of his warm jaws for a moment.

"Well get to talking my nigga, and again don't leave out shit," Devon instructed momentarily stopping.

"Ok, ok give me a sec bruh... shit that feels good... damn... oh just like that bruh...

"Spill it or I'm...," he warned.

"Aight, shit... like I said I went to the kitchen to get a snack and... man I don't even know how to start telling this shit," I said.

"You can start at the beginning and for the last time I'm telling you don't leave out a muthafuckin thing yo," Devon growled.

"Ok well, I was sleeping and woke up hungry. So since I didn't hear the music anymore I figured that everything was finished. I put on a pair of shorts and made my way towards the kitchen but when I got up there I was shocked by what I saw. Just like with me and you Ty was sitting on the sideline just watching as the two guys went at it. I'll admit it turned me on too, but out of worry that I'd be caught looking, I hauled ass back to the room. Then as I laid there hungry as fuck and now curious I decided to sneak back up there and watch from a distance. When I got back Ty was fucking the lighter skinned guy and the other one was getting head and his ass ate at the same time. Shit had my dick hard as fuck and I forgot all about being horny because I wanted in on the action. I continued watching in silence, peeping

around the corner rubbing my dick through my shorts like a perv. Then you came in just after all the cum went flying all over everybody," I explained as Devon continued feeding my needs.

"So I missed all that huh," he commented, still going strong on my joint. I could feel the climax nearing and I knew it was going to be big.

"Devon! Devon, I need you to pull the contracts up for these guys to sign and don't we have somebody else coming in," Ty yelled from up front.

"I'll be there in a minute," he shouted back just before I released my load in his mouth. It was such a relief to finally cum, but I was even hungrier now.

The Show Down

It's the Wyldcard Entertainment event of the year...

The Show Down

I couldn't believe I had actually let Devon talk me into this, but it was too late to back out now. Tonight was the night and in less than an hour it would be show time. When I told my best friend I was coming to visit I never would have dreamed this would happen. It was kind of funny though. From the time I got to Atlanta guys were hitting on me and now I was about to be the face of an all-out freak fest. Now don't get me wrong I'm definitely a freak myself but I wasn't really out with it. Only Devon and literally a handful of other dudes had tasted this dick. I wasn't on any dating apps and I didn't go out much so the only time I meet people was at church or while I'm working. Ok now before some of yall start talking about me being closeted and what not let me explain. The job I had before I came out here didn't leave much room for play and on top of that I was pretty much an unknown celebrity. So if it had got out that I was fucking dudes I don't know what would have happened. Not to mention my parents would have had heart attacks and died again.

See my parents and Devon's parents were very strict and super religious people. Devon's people were our pastors and mine were like the top elders in the church. So we were both kind of forced into the limelight of ministry, I mean Devon was even a licensed minister and I was a pretty decent musician. In fact, after I moved to Texas I landed a gig as the assistant musical director for one of the biggest churches in Houston and later became sort of a protégé to the pastor. Since I was in school I had some limits but I was still in the limelight and that as more reason than ever to keep shit low key. Now I know some of yall still probably saying this nigga on some bullshit or I ain't real but I have my reasons for handling my shit the way I do and that's that. Then I got one more for yall, and Devon don't even know this, but I just broke off an engagement with this chick I was smashing because she lied to me and said she was pregnant. Tried to catch a brother in that trap right quick. Anyway let me get back to the real shit and tell yall about the show down.

Ok so like I was saying I came to

Atlanta to visit my best friend Devon and ended up being talked into hosting this event. I agreed to do then I was a little weirded out by Devon's boss, who wanted to watch us fuck and probably more if he could have gotten his way. Shit after seeing how he auditioned the strippers I'm sure if he could have gotten his hands on my cakes he would have taken full advantage. However, that's an exit only area and from the conversation we had it's the same with him. Plus, yall remember how weird he was when he met me, but I guess that must be why they call him Ty Eros the Wyldcard. I just hope this party doesn't get too wild tonight. I do have to admit this costume looks pretty hot on me. It shows just enough to get attention but hides enough to keep the mystery. Shit niggas was thirsting after me with jeans, boots, a polo shirt, and a baseball cap on so I know I might have my hands full with this outfit. I think my body could still use some work but obviously other people thought it was sexy. I'm 5'10½, yes that half inch makes a difference, 215lbs, brown skin, and I hit the gym three to four times a week so my body is decent but I still got some work to do. You know every man has his issue with something and I just want to get bigger and more defined. Anyway I'm getting off subject again, but the outfit really did make me look good despite my flaws. It was pretty much what I came here with except for a few improvisations. So I had these ripped blue jeans that had cut outs in the front and the back. Then the top was like these straps that crisscrossed my chest and abs with two cuffs that fit around my arms. So I basically didn't have on a shirt but I was ok with that. Then in the cut out spots I had on this sheer thong type thing that tied at the waist. So my ass was showing but not all the way and my dick just kind of fell naturally into the sleeve giving a nice look at my pipe. Lastly to accent I had on a pair of tan timberland boots, red bandanas looped on the arm cuffs, and a red fitted cap. Now I ain't gon sit here and act like I'm not uncomfortable with how exposed I am, but as Devon oiled me up I couldn't help but feel kind of sexy. The way he had sucked my dick before snapping a cock ring around it had me feeling some kind of way too but it was only to get me ready. I mean I wasn't mad

*since we had been getting it in a good bit
since I got here but my dick has a mind of its
own so it is what it is now. Going into this I
had made up my mind that I wasn't gonna
fuck with anybody at this party, just flirt a bit,
do my job, and get this money. However, I
was kind of having second thoughts about that
now. Especially since I knew Rico's sexy ass
was going to be there. I definitely wanted to
get a taste of that ass and the way he flirted
with me while he was getting my shit together
let me know he wanted this dick too. Plus,
after Devon picked me up from the train
station he told me about the UPS man,
Davion, who I happened to know of through
some mutual friends. Might be nice to finally
meet him face to face if he showed up tonight.*

*I looked over at the clock and saw that
it was a quarter after seven, which meant that
the guest would soon be arriving. The workers
had already come in and were setting up in
the living area which had been transformed
into Freakville. I mean it wasn't bad, it was
just that I knew what was about to go down so
it kind of made me feel some kind of way.*

However, I had to give it to Ty and Devon though because these dudes went all out with it. I mean the loft was already a nice ass spot, but they made the space work for what they wanted for real. I could even see some dudes trying out the swing on the balcony. Before tonight I had never been to a sex party but from what I'd heard it was nothing like this. Bartenders, strippers, security, catered food, and a lavish setup that looked more like a high end slumber party rather than a freak session. It even seemed like all the workers had been handpicked too cause all of them were sexy, nicely build dudes that looked like models. Now I'll say this and I know some of you are probably thinking about it because I asked Devon this too. Why would you feed a nigga that's about to get smashed? I mean ain't that asking for somebody to get painted? Better yet ain't that asking for a fight? I know I'd be ready to break a nigga's back if he shitted on my dick. However, Devon told me that not all the dudes that come like to fuck, some just like to watch, play games, drink, and socialize so the food is there to offset the some of the alcohol. They also had extra towels, soap and douches on hand too in case of emergency. Still a bad idea to me, but I guess they knew what they were doing.

Anyway, it was almost time to get this show started and I was a bag of emotions. The adventurous and spontaneous guy in that I normally kept locked up was all eager and ready to go, but the everyday me was horny and interesting in seeing how the night would unfold but still very nervous about everything. I was definitely liking what I saw in the mirror even though I would never have put something like this together on my own. The outfit really accentuated all my good points and the oil Devon rubbed me down with made all my work in the gym pop. I hadn't seen Ty since he came in a few hours ago, fortunately Devon had all his shit together and there was minimal work left to do. I honestly think Ty was surprised that he had pulled it off with little to no help from him, other than the curveballs he threw in here and there. So far all the puzzle pieces were coming together and everything was running smoothly. Not to mention the fact that Devon had given me the run down on my role about ten times in the last hour. I understood the pressure that he was under but shit, I wasn't a pro at this either. I had never even thought about attending a sex party and now in less than thirty minutes I was going to be hosting one.

"Hey kid, it's show time, you ready?" Ty asked, peeking his head in the door.

"I'm bout as I'm gon get I guess," I replied.

"Aight well the guess will be arriving soon do I'm a need you out front to greet them as they come in," he stated, motioning for me to come out, "Listen I know your nervous cause you've never done this before but just be sexy and do what comes natural, and remember we're here with you," he continued, giving me a few words of advice as he guided me out the door.

"Ok, let's get it then," I stated, taking a deep breath before stepping out in front of him.

"You'll be good man, no worries," he

said, patting me on the back as I passed, "Hey Devon I need you to call Que and see what time he plans to roll through so we can be ready for them when they get here, he'll probably have two or three guys with him, but it's cool I've already cleared it and advised security, and good job man, everything is going good so far. By the way we have a drink and food runner for the VIP right," he added, turning his attention to Devon.

"Ok, yea we do, I handpicked the guy yesterday and confirmed that he was on board this morning, and thanks Ty," Devon answered.

"Ok make sure he's in place in about twenty minutes, and maybe have the caterer put together an extra tray or something to start us off," Ty instructed.

"It's already done, just need to get it in the room and my guy should be out front already," Devon replied.

"Ok I see you on your shit tonight, keep it up, I might let you manage more events," he said with a smile.

"Did you think my boy wouldn't come through," I asked.

"I'll admit I had my doubts, but I'm proud of my lil protégé, yall boys do good tonight I'm take yall out to breakfast in the morning and maybe I'll throw in a lil something extra on your checks. Oh and Devon, once the party is in full swing I want you relax and let the workers do what we hired them to do, maybe you and Sam could come chill in VIP with me," Ty said.

"I'll keep that in mind but you know I can't just throw my legs back relax," Devon stated.

"How come you can't I've seen you do it more than once," I chimed in.

"Don't you have a job to do Sam?" he huffed.

"Don't get mad at him because he knows you well," Ty laughed.

"Ok you know what, both yall get out of here and let me finish getting myself *together before the guest come. Because despite what you think and whatever you might have in your head over there I still have an event to supervise. Plus, Ty you know if shit start going sour you'll have my ass on a platter so if the night allows I'll peek in, but otherwise I'll be on my post," Devon said, stressing the fact that the success of this night was still in his hands.*

"Listen, I know you stressing bout doing well but you've already proven yourself to me and once the party starts and personalities mix there's things that we just won't be able to control. Now keep in mind, that niggas getting drunk and acting a fool or somebody just being an ass is the reason why we hired security, and part of our host's job is crowd control. So even if he is smashing some sexy muthafucka and some shit go down he better be ready to handle that shit," Ty explained, reiterating his contentment with the job Devon had done so far and hinting at mine.

"Well gee thanks for the free ticket to doing me," I joked.

"If he fucking he ain't gon be thinking about breaking up no fight, or mediating no issues, I already know that so I'll be keeping my eyes open, plus security better be on their shit otherwise heads gon fly and I ain't playing. Just like the guy that got caught up at the last event, I'm not having that shit at all," Devon exclaimed.

"Ok, ok well I hear the buzzer out front so that means somebody has arrived so let's get it started and we'll all do our parts to make things flow smoothly," Ty replied.

About twenty minutes later there were about ten guys in the main area and three out of the seven VIP guess had made their arrivals. My kind-hearted friend had also found a way for Darian, the stripper that didn't make the cut, to still be part of the event. Guess it might have been a crazy coincidence that he worked for the catering company they hired also, but Devon made sure he had another shot at the spotlight by using him as the runner for the VIP room. I mean he was still sexy, but I think his nerves just got to him yesterday and performing in

*front of Ty can be pretty intimidating, I guess.
Shit I wasn't exactly comfortable with him
watching me fuck either, but once I really got
in that ass I was able to block him out till he
started making suggestions and talking shit.
That me though, but anyway, we were about a
half hour into it any everything seemed to be
going smoothly. If didn't know any better, I'd
think one of the guest was one of my college
professors from Texas, but I knew for a fact
that he was married with kids and probably
had no reason to be in Atlanta. Then again
who knows these days and people can change,
though sometimes it's not actually that they
change you just never really knew them from
the beginning. So I just continued doing my
thing, mingling, chatting, greeting people, and
handling out gift bags and tickets as they
came in. By about 8:15 all the VIPs were
accounted for and from my count most of the
general party guest were present too.
However, I still hadn't seen any sign of the
UPS man and I kind of figured that he wasn't
going to show. At half pass the hour I was
supposed to officially welcome everybody and
announce the first activity. The main event*

was supposed to happen close to midnight then the rest of the night would be just straight freaking. That would also be the point when my hosting duties would be pretty much done and crowd control would be left up to security.

"Sam, everybody should be here by now, go head and make the announcement so we can really get started. By the way don't forget to show your face in VIP every now and then," Devon said, reminding me of what needed to be done, "Oh and when we get a moment you fucking me," he added.

"Ok I got it my nigga and I'll be ready," I laughed as he walked away.

"I'm serious nigga don't laugh," he snapped, turning back momentarily before continuing over to the bar.

"I got you bruh," I reiterated.

"Aight let's get it popping my nigga," he called back.

I honestly thought the shit was kind of

funny but I really laughed to shrug off the rush of nervousness that came over me. I mean we were in a room full of people and he wasn't exactly whispering when he said it. However, it wouldn't be the first time he's bullied me out of a nut so fuck it. Plus, I think his blunt words caught a few ears nearby so I instantly got a bunch of grins and stares as I made my way to the middle of the floor.

"Aight so for those who aren't already checking me out let me get your attention," I yelled as I stepped up on the platform that would later be used for the main event, "My name is B. Slayer and I'll be your host tonight so I wanted to take a second to welcome everybody to the Show Down. If you're nervous, fuck it, it's my first time doing some shit like this so shit, all us shy muthafuckas gon be getting it in tonight just like everybody else. We got some hot shit planned for the night so I'm more than sure we all gon enjoy ourselves and I don't think I need to remind yall of the rules right," I added, concluding my little speech with a general question to the group.

"No," they replied in unison.

"Aight well like I said, I'm B. Slayer so if yall need anything or have any issues come find me or talk to one of the guys you see with the staff badges hanging around their necks," I continued.

"What if I want some dick son," a slightly familiar voice yelled from the sideline.

"If the moment is right and we vibe you might get it," I laughed, nervously looking over to the direction where I hear the voice then I instantly realized who it was. Mr. UPS, Davion, had finally made his arrival and a pretty grand one at that.

"What about that ass sexy," another deep, husky voice called out.

"That ain't negotiable," I laughed as about half of the room sighed in disappointment.

"Can we at least get a good look at it since you up there," a third bassy voice inquired.

181

"Aye you can look all day my nigga just don't touch it unless you want a problem," I laughed, turning and giving the whole room an eye full of my phat black ass.

"Damn I'd love to taste them cakes," Ty exclaimed from the corner, "When you finish in here the boys in the VIP want to see you for a minute," he added.

"Aight," I was planning to do that anyway," I replied, "So now yall done seen the package, let's get to business! We got a lot of prizes to give away, contests, and don't forget the main event in a couple hours, trust me you don't want to miss that shit. We got two sexy as muthafuckas that's gon put on a live show for yall right here where I'm standing and after that it's playtime for real for real. Now if you see something you like other than myself feel free to hop on that but later on when we take the lights down that's when the real freaking gon start. Shit I might even jump in and tap some ass, but I see my nigga back there in the corner already getting domed up while I'm talking. Don't stop it's all good my man... damn he getting that shit...

my bad I got distracted yall. So anyway first thing we gon do is a biggest dick contest, so if you want to participate see my homies D-Luv and Knight Ryder over by the bar and they'll size you up and all that shit. So get your dicks hard my niggas and I'll be back in bout thirty minutes to announce the winner. Oh and yall know there's gon be a dick sucking and ass eating contest too right? I'll tell yall more about that when I come back though," I continued on trying my best to not to sound like a freaky cornball.

A few minutes later I'd made my way back to the VIP area. When I got inside I immediately noticed the lights and cameras that were focused on the king sized bed where two of the guys that came in with Que were sucking this other dude's dick. Ty and Que stood on the other side of the room talking amongst themselves, pointing and occasionally giving directions to the guys and cameramen. Rico and his partner were there too and another guy was in the far corner of the room getting his dick sucked. Moments later Darian came in with a tray of fruit and drinks, but almost dropped it when he saw the scene that was unfolding in front of us. The guy that had been getting head in the corner had now joined the other three on the bed and proceeded to slide his thick dick into the darker one's ass. I watched as he arched his back and buried his face in the other guy's thigh while his friend continued giving head. He grunted softly in a low, deep tone as ole boy began to work that ass over with slow, deep, deliberate strokes.

"Y'all are just in time," Ty exclaimed, finally acknowledging our presence, "Darian you can set that tray down over there and come join the party, and Sam if it's ok with you I'd like you to join in as well," he added.

Darian and I just looked at each other confused but obviously aware of what he wanted. The guys on the bed stared at us in anticipation of what we were going to do. Darian slowly set the tray down and looked at me as if he was waiting for me to make a move.

"I got to get back to the floor in a

minute," I stated, trying to give myself an excuse to leave.

"Just give us about ten minutes and you can go," Que chimed in.

"Aight I guess, what exactly do you want me to do," I asked.

"Well for starters, how about you come closer so he can get a better look at you," Ty suggested.

"Msn I don't know, maybe I should go finish my duties out front then come back later," I replied, looking around nervously.

It'll only take a minute I promise," Que stated, taking the initiative to meet me halfway.

"Ok just a few minutes then I need to go back out front to announce the contest winner and setup the next activity," I said.

"Trust me, I got you, it'll just be a few minutes," Que reiterated, "Do you mind if I touch you?" he asked, slowly lifting his hands to chest level.

"Nah it's cool," I answered hesitantly.

"What about the server over there, or him, him, him, or anybody else in the room," he inquired, pointing at as he spoke.

"I guess that's cool man, as long as nobody tries to fuck me or whatever we good bruh," I replied, looking around the room taking it all in as Que proceeded to feel me up.

"Damn son you got it all huh? Muscles, ass, dick, and a pretty face you're damn near perfect," he exclaimed, taking a step back.

"I wouldn't say all that, but I appreciate it bruh," I stated.

"And he's modest too… ummm Darian right," Que laughed.

"Nah it's Sam or as the patrons know me B. Slayer," I replied.

"No I'm aware of who you are I was talking to the server guy over there," Que said, pointing towards Darian.

"Yea, that's my name," Darian stated.

"Come on over here," Que instructed, beckoning to him, "I want to see if you can get him get him hard," he added as Darian stepped up closer to us.

"Uh ok," Darian agreed before dropping to his knees.

"Whoa... hold up... no offense to you my man but nah..." I exclaimed, choosing my words carefully.

"What's wrong Sam," Ty chimed in.

"Listen I'm not completely sure what's going on in here but...

"Sam, what you doing? I've been looking all over for you," Devon shrieked as he stuck his head in the door.

"I'm coming now bro," I answered, breathing a sigh of relief.

"Well hurry up we need to get this next event popping now so we can stay on schedule," he insisted.

"Ok, ok I guess I'll be back later guys," I announced as made my way towards the door.

"So I'm looking for you and you in there getting yo dick sucked nigga," Devon scolded as we walked back up the hall, "Don't even answer that I knew you were in trouble so I came to save your ass," he added, speaking just above a whisper.

"Bruh for real," I laughed.

"What? I know how those dudes are and Ty ain't as slick as he thinks he is either," Devon said.

"What do you mean?" I asked.

"You saw all those lights and shit in there, he trying to put together a new movie project but think I don't know it, and from the looks of it him and Que had plans on including you," he answered.

"Yea I bet he did," I stated, giving a cold stare back in the direction of Ty's suite.

Once back out front I went on with my

duties, mingling and making sure everybody was having a good time. It was kind of funny the way the guys would sneak in a little feel here and there. In fact, the dude that won the biggest dick contest wanted yo feel on my ass instead of taking the trophy. I wasn't really feeling the idea but I agreed and in return he had to suck my dick. So it was kind of a win, win situation, he got to feel my ass and I got some head. I was actually surprised at how good he did it and I would have let him suck me off, but after two other guys jumped in and started licking my nipples and grabbing my ass too I had to stop it all. I'll admit it felt good, but I didn't want to be the buffet for a room full of horny niggas. Eventually somebody would have crossed the line so it had to end before it got ugly.

"Aight yall that's enough," I announced, pushing everybody off me.

"Damn bruh that dick taste good as fuck," our prize winner moaned, reluctantly giving up his lollipop.

"That mouth felt good too my nigga,

maybe later I'll let you finish," I replied.

"Aight so can we get some chairs on the stage for our judges," Devon shouted across the room, "Let's keep this shit moving," he added.

"Ok so while they getting setup I need all my headmasters to step forward! If you think you got skills with that mouth and that throat come on up here and show our judges what you working with," I announced, "So this is how this shit gon work, make sure you listening because I'm only gonna say it once. You will have one minute with each judge, if you can't deep throat don't even come up here, if the judge feels teeth you'll be disqualified and there's no exceptions! So like I said one minute with each of our judges, after that minute you'll move on to the next, if your jaws get tired just go head and sit back down or don't come up. I see we have seven up here, can we get one more of yall to step up? Nobody? Ok, let's make this interesting... humm... if I can get one more participant I'll sit in as a judge myself," I stated, realizing I might have been setting myself up.

"If that's the case I'm in," said the man who I had assumed to be a familiar face, "I've always wondered how that body looked and I'm definitely not disappointed at all," he added.

"Well... I..."

"Guess that settles it, get another chair on the stage let's get the first four contestants up here," Devon chimed in.

"Yea let's get started," I said, recovering from my shock.

"So like B. Slayer said yall will each have one minute to give the best head you can to the judge," Devon stated.

Five minutes later the first round of the contest was over and the next group was taking their places. So far I hadn't been impressed by any of them, but hopefully that would change in the next few minutes. I was still kind of surprised to find out that my old professor, Dr. Tierre Collins, messed around with dudes. Then to top it off he was moments away from sucking my dick. The man who had been somewhat of a mentor to me throughout my undergrad years was on his knees about to suck my dick. It was so surreal to me that I couldn't even focus on the guys before him. Then when the moment finally came it was like a dream that I almost didn't want to wake up from. His lips were so soft, gently caressing my pipe and drawing it into his warm mouth, effortlessly taking it down his throat. I'm not easily impressed but I was definitely mystified by the skill he displayed. Yes, I said mystified because I never would have imagined that he was down, let alone give amazing head. In all my life there had only been a handful of people that could deep throat me and do it well. When our minute was over I was almost tempted not to let him go, but of course I had to play it cool.

"That mouth was a beast huh bruh," J-Roc, the judge sitting next to me laughed.

"Bruh..." I sighed, throwing my head back in awe.

"If the others agree it may seem that we have a winner but to be fair we got to do

another round with the best out of the eight,"
he replied.

"I definitely agree son," D-Luv
interjected.

"Well he's got three votes, I'm ready to
call it," I laughed.

"Four votes, but Mr. Big dick and the
light skinned guy with fat ass were good too in
my book," Rico added.

"Ok, ok so what yall want to do,"
Devon inquired.

"I say we be fair like J-Roc said and
get the best ones back up here and decide
from them," I replied.

"Yea I'm good with that," D-Luv
concurred.

"Me too," Rico added.

"Ok so yall want to bring back,"
Devon asked.

"Well ole school is definitely in!" J-
Roc exclaimed.

"I want Big Dick and red too," Rico stated.

"Aight that's three, who else yall want?" Devon inquired.

"How about the buff dude with the dreads," J-Roc suggested.

"He was ok, but I guess he was better than the other ones and at least two of them gagged on my shit," I added, trying to recall them all.

"Aight, so it seems like we might have a winner, but the judges are still deliberating," Devon announced, "If you gagged, and you know who you are, you're disqualified so step on back. We have three frontrunners so far and they're discussing a fourth so out of the five yall that are still standing up here, four of yall will get another chance to show the judges what you can do," he continued.

"Aye D we ready," I stated.

"Ok so our judges have made a

decision... Tierre, Jason, Calvin, and Frankie... yall have been selected to go for another round. This time yall will have two minutes on each dick. If you manage to make one of them pop I that qualifies as an instant win right yall," Devon declared, looking back at us.

"I don't even think our agreed leader could make me cum in two minutes bruh," D-Luv boasted.

"Ahh ok, so contestants yall have a challenge, let's get this shit started and see what happens," Devon said, beckoning for the guys to take their places.

About a minute into the round the room was quiet with anticipation. Low grunts and moans could be heard here and there as our contestants turned up to the heat. First up to serve me was Calvin aka Mr. Big Dick, whose skills I'd had the pleasure of experiencing just before the contest started. He was good but compared to Tierre it was... well... I'll just say there wasn't much to compare other than how soft both their lips were. Next was Jason aka Buff Dreads, he wasn't really all that in my opinion, but he had this trick he did with his tongue that felt real nice. After him came Frankie, better known as Red Cakez, the deep throat master. Frankie, in my mind, was Tierre's main competition and that pretty ass was just begging for some dick. I definitely had my inhibitions about this event but as the night unfolded my reservations were fleeting. I'd never been one to flaunt my sexuality but somehow I was comfortable here. Maybe part of that was because I was somewhat in control of the whole situation. Then again it could just be a part of me that I'd been suppressing and now it was getting its chance to live. Either way I finally had Tierre back in front of me and it was evident that he was hungry for the prize. Gazing into my eyes with unbridled concupiscence as he took my pulsing dick down his throat. I bit down on my bottom lip and attempted to steady my breaths as I grasped desperately at my composure. It was a losing battle, but my pride wasn't going to allow me to give in easily. Still a climax was growing near and my fight was becoming futile.

"Aight times up fellas!" Devon exclaimed, unknowingly saving my ass, "Contestants let go of the dicks and step off the stage while our judges make their final decision," he added.

"He almost got you didn't he," J-Roc laughed.

"Between his mouth and your moans when Frankie got to your ass I don't which one was turning me on more," I countered.

"Oh really... well the night is still young my dude so I guess we'll have to see what else I can do to turn you on," he replied with a smile.

"You'll have to stand in line homie," Devon interjected.

"Come on yall we need to make this decision, yall can debate about who gon freak with B. Slayer later," Rico added, attempting to play mediator.

"Yea you're right, so my vote is still for Tierre and if I had to choose a second I'd say

Frankie, " J-Roc replied.

"I'd say Frankie, then Tierre, " Rico stated.

"My vote is for Tierre, Frankie is good, but Tierre almost made me nut both times, " D-Luv said, adding his thoughts to the discussion.

"Ok B. Slayer that leaves you to decided, you can either tie it or give us a winner, " Devon weighed in, "No pressure though bro, " he added.

"Yea sure, no pressure at all, " I laughed nervously.

"If it's any help just remember that these guy's future isn't on the line here, " Rico joked.

"Ok, ok I just never had to do this before yall so I'm a lil anxious about it. now in my mind there is definitely a clear winner, but... I'm not completely comfortable with admitting that either and I... "

"Bro, bro take a minute, take a breath,

and relax I can see that there's obviously something bothering you but right now I need you to pull it together and let's make the best of this situation and we can talk about whatever is going on later," Devon interrupted cutting me off before I went any further.

"Exactly what is going on guys," Ty inquired as he approached the platform with Que on his heels.

"Our judges are deliberating about the contest and B. Slayer's decision will be the deciding factor but he's having a little trouble with it," Devon explained.

"I see... so B. Slayer what's up, you got four guys over there waiting for a decision and a room full of spectators waiting to see which one of these dudes they might be able to get some good head from later tonight. Now I watched a lil bit of the contest on closed circuit so I know you got somebody in mind," Ty stated, staring at me coldly.

"I vote for Tierre and Frankie, there's no issue, I just had to think about it for a

minute," I replied, staring directly into his eyes.

"Ok then, we have his choices go head and move forward with that Devon," Que instructed.

"You suggesting that we go another round with the two finalist?" Rico asked.

"Nah but if the rest of yall have made choices you can move forward the votes you have and make cuts based on that," Que answered.

"That should give B. Slayer time to make a final decision and then Rico I need you to come back and get ready for the main event. We gon push the timeline a bit. So once this is finished make sure everybody has their ticket and then get the raffle going. Then after that's done we'll be ready for the main event to start," Ty chimed in.

"Ok then..."

"Don't trip D, we just want to move things along so yall can come chill in the VIP

with us," Que stated, cutting Devon off before he could object to the change.

"Yea ok I got it," Devon said as he prepared to make the announcement.

"Yo D I..."

"Don't worry about it B. Slayer," he snapped, cutting me off, "Aight yall we halfway to a decision," he continued, addressing the guests.

"B. Slayer after you finish with raffles and announce the main event, I'd like for you to report back to the VIP room. Que and I have somebody we want you to meet," Ty started before walking off.

Ten minutes later deliberations were over and Tierre was named the headmaster of the night. For his prize he was given a small novelty trophy shaped like an open mouth and an invitation to the VIP room. Devon didn't say too much, but I could tell he wasn't happy with Ty and Que changing his plans. I might have been a little in the doghouse too but who can think straight when you're getting head *from your mentor? Seeing him walk in here was one thing then to have him admit to secretly admiring me and lastly give me one of the best blowjobs ever was too much for me. Even though I had previously been warming up to my environment I was almost ready to retreat back into my conservative shell at that point. However, the bus was rolling now and if I didn't rise the occasion I'd have two mad pit bulls at my throat. So I did what I had to do and pulled through for Devon's sake and mine.*

Over the next thirty minutes we raffled off everything from games, sex toys and gift cards, to dates with porn stars and the VIP guest. One of the prizes was this huge life-like dildo and the dude that won it looked like he would be split in half just thinking about using it. Shit looked like it was two of my dick put together and about maybe two inches longer. I couldn't imagine that shit going in somebody's ass but I guess it was possible for somebody. A few of the guys wanted to raffle me off but Devon wasn't having that at all. I mean I wasn't in agreement either but you would have thought I was his man the way he jumped up and put them dudes in line. Or so he thought, honestly I don't think many of them paid him any mind. However, Sam aka B. Slayer was still not being raffled off to anybody, and after this last prize is announced it'll be time for the main event.

"Sam I need to talk to you after you introduce Rico and Quinn," Devon whispered in my ear before stepping down from the platform.

"Ok..." I replied hesitantly, already knowing what this was going to be about, "So what's up yall feeling the scene tonight?" I exclaimed, turning my attention back to the crowd. There were a few responses while others just keep doing what they were doing, but I took their preoccupation as a yes and proceeded on.

"I want to taste that dick," a voice yelled back.

"Me too," cried another before I could respond to the first.

"Yall just hang tight and you might just get the chance to do that. Now that we've gotten all the games out the way it's time to get to the business. Even though I see some of yall couldn't wait but that's cool yall came here to get that good nut on the low and then go back to your normal lives with no strings attached right? Exactly so let's add some more gas to this fire and... you know what... come on up here," I said, switching gears midstream, "You come on up here," I reiterated beckoning to the loud mouth in the back of the room that was so eager to taste my dick. Devon was probably gonna have a fit but oh well. I needed to revive myself from the little emotional fumble I had earlier. So once again I was throwing caution to the wind and allowing this random guy to suck my dick in front of everybody. "While they finish setting up anybody else that wants to taste this dick get in line behind my friend right here," I added, placing my free hand on the guy's shoulder while I released my flaccid pipe from its sleeve for the second time.

"I've had my taste already I want that

shit in me son," Tierre boasted.

"I wouldn't mind that either," Frankie chimed in.

"One step at a time y'all," I laughed, realizing the can of worms I just opened.

"The stage will be ready in two minutes sir," one of the workers informed me.

"Aight, y'all heard that you got two minutes to get up here and taste this dick before we move on," I stated as my conscience started to remind me of how randomly insane I was being.

"Well I ain't tripping, if not tonight, I'll get that dick one day," Tierre said before taking a step back.

"Ok! Well while he's sucking my dick... damn son, why weren't you in the contest... shit! Anyway, we bout to have two sexy ass muthafuckas hit this stage and turn all the way up for yall. Now I don't want to give too much away but it's about to go down... damn this dude mouth is like pussy," I moaned

while trying to set the scene for the main event, but I was clearly distracted by dude's skill, "Ok homie, let the next guy get a taste," I added, pulling my dick away from him.

"We're good to go bro," the worker informed me.

"Ok hit the lights, que the music, and let's get it popping bruh," I exclaimed, pulling my dick away from the guy that had just barely gotten his lips wrapped around it.

"Damn I ain't even get to taste it good bruh," he whined.

A few minutes later the only lights on in the room were a pair of spotlights that were pointed at the stage. Rico and Quinn were making their ways around it, seductively teasing the audience and each other as the lights followed them. The song playing was slow and sensual but the energy in the room was running high. Looked like my boy had done good picking these two and of course Ty had to literally put his stamp on them. So since my audience was occupied I took the opportunity to find Devon and see what he wanted. Hopefully it wasn't to lecture me or one of his jealous fits. I mean we've never officially been a couple, but I guess there was always something there between us pass the friendship. So there have been times when one of us would get a little jealous about shit. Again we weren't in a relationship but we had an understanding I guess.

"What's up bruh," I asked, finding Devon behind the bar.

"Shit giving the bartender a break right now, but umm... here's your grenade... I just wanted to know what happened up there, and no I'm not worried about them dudes sucking yo dick. I knew certain things would be likely to happen... two more, ok... when I asked you to take the job I knew something might happen... yea I got you bro," he replied, serving and taking orders as we talked.

"Umm ok, well..."

"I'm back, thanks for covering for me D," Mike, the bartender, said.

"No problem, let make sure to stay on

top of those orders and let me know if you need anything else," Devon answered, "So tell me what's up bruh," he continued, turning his attention back to me.

"You might think this is funny but Tierre was one of my instructors in Texas and up till now I thought he was straight," I replied.

"Son you know how many alleged straight men are in this bitch," he laughed.

"Yea I do but it's different with him bro," I stated.

"Sam who is this man for real bro," Devon asked, noticing how uncomfortable I was getting talking about him.

"I told you he..."

"Yea he was one of your teachers, but there's something else isn't it," he questioned before I could repeat myself.

"I've been to this man's house, ate dinner with his wife and kids, went to his church and watched him worship, he looked

*out for me when I needed shit... he was
like..."*

*"I get it don't say any more bro, if you
want me to ask him to leave I can," Devon
interrupted.*

*"No, no, no don't do that it just threw
me because I didn't expect that and to find out
he's been attracted to me all this time on top
of that. I just... it was just too much to process
at one time," I said.*

*"Ok so you good now bruh? Oh wait a
minute, you tripping because you had a lil
thing for him too then he sucked that dick and
blew your mind huh," he joked, not knowing
how true his words were.*

*"Shut up man, you always got to make
a joke about shit," I snapped.*

*"Aww you feeling some kind of way
now," he laughed.*

*"Man you tripping, I'm going make
another round then I'm done for the night if
that's ok with you and our porn mogul back*

there," I stated as I walked away.

"Come on bro," Devon called behind me.

"I'll see you in the VIP room," I yelled back.

I walked around for a minute sulking because I didn't expect the reaction I got from him. Then again Devon does know me better than anyone else. Maybe he was just trying to lighten the mood by cracking a joke. Still in joking he had said something that I was afraid to admit myself. In the time we'd spent together I had gained a little attraction to him. Then to come here and find out that he'd been peeping me out too. Then on top of that his head game was something serious for real. Anyway, it was a lot to take in and I wasn't ready for any of it.

"Can I get a good taste of that dick now?" the guy who I'd deprived of tasting it earlier asked.

"Give me a minute man, I promise I got you, just give me a minute," I replied.

"Ok I'll be looking for you bruh," he said.

"Trust me man I know, and I got you son, I got you," I assured him as my attention was captured by the activity on stage. The erotic dance had turned into straight out foreplay. In a sixty-nine position with Quinn on top they showed the whole room just how sexy sucking dick and eating ass could be. The way Quinn effortlessly deep throated Rico's pipe nearly made Frankie and Tierre look like amateurs. Rico wasn't playing with that ass either, slithering his tongue in, out, and around that hole with expert precision that you could see all over Quinn's face. Almost made me want to pull my dick out hop on stage with them. As I looked around a few of our guests were actively engaged in the moment as well. Most were front and center watching the action while others were kissing, feeling each other up, and maybe one or two couples were already busy sucking and licking themselves. Devon was occupied with the bar and settling things with caterers since all that was being wrapped for the night. I didn't

figure too many people would be focused on eating anything anyway but I was proved wrong. So I was also sure now that the enemas and douches that had been purchased would be used as well, hopefully. Like I said earlier no top likes to be painted, at least I don't, and any bottom with any kind of decency keeps it clean. I've only had maybe one or two experiences with that and I'll just say it didn't end well.

I continued walking around the room for about another five minutes or so scoping things out. This was definitely something new for me but I was low key liking it. Even with the uncomfortable moments, this experience was something I'd be willing to have more often. As my eyes meandered around I did my best not to lock gazes with anyone for too long. Though I may have been getting comfortable I still didn't want too much attention. Being the host I think I had enough spotlight on me so I certainly didn't want to give anybody the wrong idea. Oh and let's not forget about the stunt Que tried to pull earlier. Those crazy porn directors thought they were about to have me mixed up in some shit but thank goodness for Devon barging in when he did. My way of getting out of the situation may not have been best for any of us. I don't think Darian really wanted to be involved like that either, however, I do believe that he was going with it because he was hungry for some kind of success. He had previously been rejected and now since he had a second chance he was probably willing to do whatever it took now. That said, I don't think I've even seen him since I left out of there.

So anyway, I'm sure yall wondering what's going on, on stage and when or if I'm going back in the VIP. Well here's the answer to both of those questions right here. First off I have no choice but to go back in the VIP, but I'll get to that in a bit. Second, Rico and Quinn were giving the room a replay of what I saw a day ago minus Ty. That phat ass of Quinn's jiggled like jelly as he rode Rico's dick like a pro. The guys near the stage chanted lustfully and cheered them on with occasional feel or smack on the ass. Quinn didn't seem to mind the added attention so I paid it no mind either. After all I was off duty at this point anyway, yet I still felt like there needed to be some crowd control. So I walked up there and admonished our frisky gentlemen to keep their distance. I got a few dirty looks but having security take a seat on the edge of the stage showed that I meant business. I hated to be a buzz kill but hell everybody knows you don't touch the strippers, even though I was tempted myself. Seeing them in action up close and personal reminded me of how bad I wanted to join in during their audition yesterday. However, I fought the urge follow my instincts and just sat quietly on the edge of stage where I could get a front row view. Quinn's moans triggered memories of how he'd begged to be fucked harder the day before. Letting my mind wander I'd unconsciously began rubbing my own dick. "Pull that shit out and stroke it bruh," I heard a raspy voice cry out, alerting me that I was attracting attention and letting Quinn and Rico know I was there. Catching a glimpses of the security guard on one side and me on the other they kicked into overdrive. For a second

I locked eyes with Quinn and in that moment I knew I had to tap that ass before the night ended. Not to mention Rico had already made his intentions known so it was a deal.

"Fuck you nigga!" somebody yelled across the room.

"Get yo shit and get the fuck out," I heard Devon shout back as the room feel silent.

"Bitch ass wannabe how the fuck you gon put me out," the irate guy snapped back, "Yall muthafuckas should glad I came to this ratchet ass freak show, he added.

"Hey man, just keep it cool and do as you were asked. There's no need to make a scene," one of the security guards interjected.

"Man fuck you, you ain't shit either," the guy continued to rant.

"No I believe the word is fuck you, now get out of my house before I toss yo ass out personally," Ty chimed in emerging from the hallway in all his naked glory.

"Man look, all I was trying to do was help the man get his nut," the guy tried to explain.

"But he didn't want your help and you tried to force yourself on him and would have succeeded if we didn't pull you off him," Devon interrupted.

"Where's the other one," Ty asked, his dick swinging like a bat as he made his way through.

"He's in the bathroom," the security guard replied.

"Aight I'm a go check on him, yall get this sad muthafucka out of here and since my shit is ratchet son I'm a make sure you find out just how ratchet I can be," Ty stated stepping in the dude's face, "I should beat the fuck out of yo bitch ass, but I'm a be cool and I'm a go back to my room and finish what I was doing before I was interrupted by this bullshit as stunt you tried to pull. Then on second though... now I feel better," Ty added, turning away as spoke but then turning back *and punching the dude square in the jaw. I figured Ty probably had a nasty tempter, but I was still surprised to him knock that dude out. Then on top of they just threw him and all his shit out on the street. I mean it's actually kind of funny in retrospect, but I'm sure he wasn't laughing when he woke up. Not to mention he'd been thrown on the street butt ass naked in downtown Atlanta. He could have been robbed, picked up by the police, or anything could have happened between the time he was put out and when he woke up. However, I guess that was a small cost to pay for what he did.*

After all that was over Ty and the dude came back out and he made announcement reiterating the no means no policy and using old boy as an example of what can happen if the rule was broken, I think he was more pissed about homeboy insulting his brand and also trying to protect Devon. I could be wrong but hell Ty might have been weird and freaky, but I could tell he really cared about everybody's safety. Especially his number one employee and protégé Devon. Anyway, after the dust had settled everybody went back to having a good time. Rico and Quinn invited Davion aka Mr. UPS on stage and that really got the show going. They tried to involve me a little but after seeing Devon deal with that lil confrontation I wanted to go make sure he was ok. So after I found the other guy that I promised I'd let suck my dick, I caught up with Devon and ducked off in the guest room so we could talk.

"Man did you see how that muthafucka was literally trying to rape that man," Devon said once the door was closed and locked.

"Nah I missed that, but I did hear when he yelled fuck you nigga," I replied, dropping down on the bed.

"Yea he tried to shine after he got called on that shit," he laughed.

"Yea I'm surprised you weren't the one to knock that nigga's lights out," I joked.

"A few seconds longer and I might have been, but Ty took care of that," he

continued to laugh, taking a seat next to me.

"Yea he did, I didn't expect that though, shit I didn't expect to see him at all. It's like he just popped up out of nowhere," I replied.

"He has a way of doing that sometimes, but his timing is always pretty good, like tonight," Devon said.

"I definitely can agree with that, but shit I just wanted to make sure you were good man," I stated.

"Oh yea bruh, I'm good niggas try shit like that all the time, most of them are just jealous because of the position I have or mad because they didn't make the cut. Them dudes don't phase me though, shit is insignificant man," he said, shaking his head.

"I see, and speaking of not making the cut I see you pulled some strings for Darian," I replied with a smile.

"Nigga what you grinning for, I only helped him out because I knew he really

needed a gig. I might be Ty's protégé but I don't dip in the cookie jar like that," he snapped.

"Ok, ok I wasn't saying all that I just thought it was nice of you to help that man out," I stated, lifting my hands in surrender.

"Uh huh, well I was just letting you know nigga, because I know how you think and just in case you were wondering yes Ty and I have fucked," Devon blurted out unexpectedly.

"Well damn, thanks for the confession and I guess you and Davion was just an accident this morning huh," I laughed.

"You know what... it was and I don't regret it either. That was some good ass dick," he answered.

"It was huh," I said smugly.

"Yep it sure was, had my ass creaming and cumming like a muthafucka bruh," he continued, knowing that I was low key jealous.

"Ok you can spare me all the details bruh," I huffed, starting to get a little irritated.

"Well it's only the truth but I will say nobody fucks me like you do," Devon said with sly grin.

"Oh now you want to stroke my ego after telling how good somebody else fucked you," I griped.

"I'm serious, Davion and Ty have nice sized dicks and pretty good stroke games, but they aren't you. We have history and there's a feeling that only you can make me feel. With us it's not just good dick to me or some ass to you, it's deeper than that. I know I might sound like I'm just spouting out a bunch of mushy bullshit but I'm serious. Shit to be honest I've loved you for a long time bruh, and I mean that you're more than just a friend to me... I'm a stop there though before I make a fool of myself," he stated.

"I don't think it's bullshit, I mean Ty even saw that there was a certain chemistry

between us. I just think we've always had certain feelings for each other but never crossed that line for fear of losing each other. Now I'm starting to sound like the emotional sap," I laughed.

"A little bit, but you're right and maybe one day we'll stop being scared and make that move," Devon said.

"Yea maybe so," I reiterated.

"Uh huh so until then why don't you come up out that costume and fuck me like you love me," he suggested, tugging at the tie on my waist.

"You put this shit on me, so you can take it off," I stated, laying back on the bed.

"I don't have a problem with that," Devon replied.

About two hours later the most of the guest had left except for a few stragglers that were still trying to get a nut. Ty and his crew had wrapped up whatever craziness was going on in the VIP and everybody but Que was gone. Devon and I had just finished our own personal freak session so I was waiting for my turn in the bathroom so I could take a shower. While I waited I took a stroll around the front room just to check things out. The cleaning crew would be coming in the morning, but there honestly wasn't much to be cleaned. There were a few towels here and there, condom wrappers, drink cups, and the mats that had been laid down to protect the floor. We really could have cleaned up ourselves, but I guess Ty had his reasons for wanting a professional cleaning. I sat on the stage and watched the three guys that were still going at it. After a minute of gazing into the dark corner I realized who the guys were. That pretty red plump ass could only belong to Frankie, Mr. Red Cakez himself, and there was no mistaking Davion's muscular build and distinct voice. The other guy that was fucking Frankie hadn't had much interaction with me during the night but I remembered the tats on his arm. Tierre had been sucking his dick earlier while I was giving my introduction. He was pretty nice looking dude, average body, nice ass, and from what I could tell a nice stroke game. I wanted to sample that ass myself but I figured there would be plenty opportunity to do so in the coming weeks. Then just as dude started spraying his load over Frankie's ass Devon was tapping me on the shoulder to let me know that I could use the bathroom now. I slowly got up and made my way to the bathroom, keeping my eyes glued to that corner as Davion mounted that ass. The moans the echoed through the loft were indicative of what Devon had said earlier, but I was more interested in getting those cakes. I'd heard some shit about Davion from some mutual friends and tonight proved that he was a bona fide freak just like they said.

Once in the bathroom I could still hear the commotion of muffled moans and shit talk. I also heard Ty amidst all of it telling them that the party was over and they needed to wrap it up. Then there was a knock on the door just as I stepped into the shower.

Sam when you finish, we gon go get some food," Ty's voice called from the other side.

"Aight cool, I won't be long," I yelled back.

As the warm water enrobed my body I recalled the events of the night and the crazy days leading up to it. From the moment I stepped off the train I knew I was in for a ride. The guys hitting on me while I navigated my way to the loft, Devon with his proposition, Ty walking in on us then watching us fuck, the threesome Ty had with Rico and Quinn, and then finally tonight. I mean what can I really say about this night to sum it up. This was definitely an experience for me but in a way it was nothing like what I'd expected. There were still some uncomfortable moments but overall I actually enjoyed it. Especially that private session with Devon. We'd had sex plenty times before but something was very different about tonight. Maybe it was finally coming to terms with how we felt about each other, I don't know, but it was undeniably hot. I almost felt like I was losing something as the water rinsed away the remnants of the night.

However, I was sure there would be a replay and I was definitely going to be in the house. So after lathering myself up and rising off for the last time, I turned off the water, grabbed a towel, wrapped it around my waist, and made my way out of the bathroom. I looked around in disappointment to see that our stragglers had left. Devon and Ty had gotten dressed and were sitting at the bar talking. I let them know that I was done showering and just needed a few minutes to get dressed.

Twenty minutes later we were all in Ty's truck heading to IHOP to get some food and discuss the event. As we rode Ty told us about how Tierre had been the star of the show when he got to the VIP room, but refused to sign the release form when he realized he was being filmed. I completely understand his reasons for not wanting any record of the night's event to get out. However, it left Ty with the task of either editing out and footage that showed his face or omitting it completely. He also admitted that he wanted me to be a part of the production but after seeing how uncomfortable I was when I came in he didn't push the issue much. He actually found it funny that I never came back. Yet there was still an offer for me to do a scene but I had to sleep on that. Apparently Que really liked my look and Ty had vouched for my sexual prowess, but again I wasn't so sure about that. I came to Atlanta to spend some time with my boy not make a career in porn. As interesting and financially appealing as it seemed I just couldn't deal with the thought of somebody from home seeing it and blasting my business to the world. On the flip side, I was down with hosting or even just attending another show down.

Trapped

*I take a step forward and I'm pushed
back three
I win small victories but still, every
time, I lose the battle
It's a vicious cycle that keeps me
tightly bound in its claws
My freedom is joke exasperated by my
addiction to life
The thorn that's been deeply embedded
into my flesh
Like Superman's kryptonite it cripples
my burning flesh
A bed of quicksand that pulls me
deeper with every move I make
Locked away in the prison of my own
twisted desires
My wrists are shackled, ankles
strapped with chains
There's no denying or fighting the
painful truth*
I'M TRAPPED!

Ty Eros